Diary of
Steve and the Wimpy Creeper

An Unofficial Minecraft Series

FULL TRILOGY

Diary of Steve and the Wimpy Creeper – Book 1
Diary of Steve and the Wimpy Creeper – Book 2
Diary of Steve and the Wimpy Creeper – Book 3

Skeleton Steve

www.SkeletonSteve.com

Copyright

"Diary of Steve and the Wimpy Creeper Trilogy"

"Diary of Steve and the Wimpy Creeper – Book 1"

"Diary of Steve and the Wimpy Creeper – Book 2"

"Diary of Steve and the Wimpy Creeper – Book 3"

Published in the United States of America by Lightbringer Media LLC, 2017

To join Skeleton Steve's free mailing list, for updates about new Minecraft Fanfiction titles:

www.SkeletonSteve.com

Table of Contents

Contents

Book Introduction
by Skeleton Steve

Love MINECRAFT? ***Over 37,000 words of kid-friendly fun!***

This high-quality fan fiction fantasy diary book is for kids, teens, and nerdy grown-ups who love to read epic stories about their favorite game!

Thank you to <u>all</u> of you who are buying and reading my books and helping me grow as a writer. I put many hours into writing and preparing this for you. I *love* Minecraft, and writing about it is almost as much fun as playing it. It's because of *you*, reader, that I'm able to keep writing these books for you and others to enjoy.

This book is dedicated to *you*. Enjoy!!

After you read this book, please take a minute to leave a simple review. I really appreciate the feedback from my readers, and love to read your reactions to my stories, good or bad. If you ever want to see your name/handle featured in one of my stories, leave a review and *tell me about it* in there! And if you ever want to ask me any questions, or tell me your idea for a cool Minecraft story, you can email me at steve@skeletonsteve.com.

Are you on my **Amazing Reader List**? Find out at the end of the book!

September the 12ᵗʰ, 2016

For those of you who love Steve and Cree and like a good deal, enjoy this Box Set! If you'd like to see me continue the adventures of Steve and Cree, please let me know in the comments!

P.S. - Have you joined the <u>Skeleton Steve Club and my Mailing List</u>??

You found one of my diaries!!

Some of these books are my own stories, and some are the tales of the friends I've made along the way. And a precious few of my books, like this one, are from my "Fan Series", which means that it's a book I worked on *together* with one of my fans! Make sure to let me *and the fan who helped* me know if you like our book!

This story is from the *Diamond55* Fan Series. It takes place on a Minecraft world, much like my own Diamodia, where Steve and his friends call themselves *Minecraftians*.

What you are about to read is the COLLECTION of Steve and the Wimpy Creeper, books 1-3. Enjoy!

Be warned—this is an *epic book!* You're going to *care* about these characters. You'll be scared for them, feel good for them, and feel bad for them! It's my hope that you'll be *sucked up* into the story, and the adventure and danger will be so intense, you'll forget we started this journey with a *video game!*

With that, readers, I present to you the full tale of **Steve and the Wimpy Creeper.**

Box Set Book 1:
Diary of Steve
and the Wimpy Creeper 1

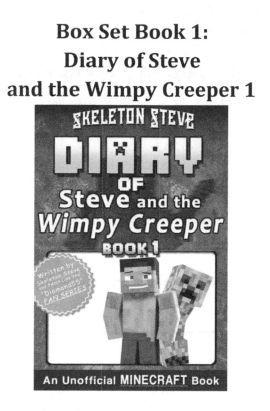

Steve was lonely.

Alex and the other Minecraftians just wanted to spend all of their time adventuring and fighting mobs, but Steve was happy to just stay home in his quiet village, tending to his crops and taking care of his animals.

But Steve's calm, lonely life was in for a big BOOM of a change when he was approached one day by a gentle creeper that wouldn't explode, who he named Cree. Would Steve find the friendship he was looking for in Cree? Or would the creeper coming into his life lead to too much adventure and excitement for him to handle?

Day 1

Well first off, I'm Steve! I'm a human! A pretty cool human, too. I may not be the strongest like my friend Alex, or the most adventurous, but I have some awesome crops and cows!

Today started off pretty normal. I usually ate breakfast, though sometimes I forgot, and then I went outside to feed my farm animals. It was just another ordinary morning.

I stood up and stretched, sighing deeply. That was a good night's sleep! There was hardly any *mob* noise outside overnight, and the cows stayed calm. I looked around my cabin, smiling.

Aah . . . Perfect.

Thud, Thud, Thud, on the window.

What was that? I looked around and laughed.

Right! I almost forgot to mention, but I have an entire *village* to myself!

Well, *almost* to myself. There *were* villagers. And when I looked outside, there was a villager running into my window as if he was stuck.

"Again? Haha."

I may as well help the villager, so he doesn't break my glass, I thought.

I went outside and turned him around, walking him away from the cabin so he didn't accidentally turn back. The confused villager walked on to the village square. I turned to look at my crops, cows and chickens, and I smiled wide.

It was so nice.

My cows *moo-ed* and my chickens *bawk bawked*.

Back inside my cabin, I suddenly felt *lonely*. The sadness surprised me, but I was determined to cheer myself up.

"No reason to be sad!" I told myself.

I had my cows and my chickens. The villagers were not too bad either, but I didn't have any friends.

Not really.

There were *others* like me, but those guys liked to go out into the wilderness to fight all of the mobs, and I didn't. I liked harvesting my wheat and sitting out on the bay.

Before the loneliness bothered me too much, I snapped myself out of it, and got dressed. I had chores to do!

"Energy, Steve! Energy!" I muttered to myself.

Yes, I realize it, and you'll see it soon too, but I guess I *talk to myself* a lot. That's what happens when your only friends are cows and chickens.

I changed into my normal farm clothes and went outside. First, I harvested some wheat and replanted what I had taken out. Then, I went over to my cows and chickens and fed them. The cows *moo-ed* and the chickens *bawk bawked* as they happily flocked around their breakfasts.

My animal friends were really fun to watch, and I smiled. One of the chickens looked up at me, as if asking me a question.

Bawk bawk!

"What's wrong, little chicken? Not enough food?"

Bawk bawk!

The water dish was empty.

"Doh!" I smacked myself in the forehead. "I forgot, sorry!"

"See, this is what happens when you get distracted," I told myself as I walked to the well. The town's water supply was at the center of my village, and I could see all the other villagers *hurrring* and *humming* just as I dipped the bucket in. They all turned to look at me, and I waved at them.

"Morning, fellas!" I said.

They just stared back, furrowing their brows and pressing their lips together, like they normally did.

One of the villagers came up to me and looked down at the water.

"Oh, what was that?" I asked.

The villager hadn't *said* anything, but I wanted someone to talk to. I know it's weird but, *hey*, at least I can talk about something, even if I can't understand them, and they probably don't understand me.

"Yeah, I had a good night too. Thank you for asking!"

He still hadn't looked up at me, but I talked on.

"Yup! Pretty quiet, I do say! The monsters . . . have . . ."

The villager walked away, like they normally did after a few minutes.

"Alright, buddy! Good talking to you too! See you later!"

I grabbed the bucket, held it against me, and turned around again to the group of villagers still hovering around.

"Later, guys! No, sorry—I can't stay! I've got *chores* to do!"

I waved at the villagers and walked away.

Yes, weird—I know. But they were the only people around me most of the time that I could interact with on a normal basis! The other Minecraftians were usually out fighting mobs and exploring dangerous places—not my idea of fun! So, I usually spent my time tending to the village, collecting food, and taking care of my animals.

Bawk bawk!

Moo!

"Yes, yes, I know you guys have been waiting!" I said.

My animal friends were frustrated with me because I took so long gathering water. But to be honest, it wasn't my fault at all! It was that villager—he just wouldn't stop talking to me about how his evening went!

"The nerve of some people!" I said to my thirsty cow.

Moooooo!

Well, he clearly didn't believe me, but I tried. Ha ha. And that was when it happened—the incident that turned my very calm and normal life completely topsy-turvy!

There was a sudden loud noise from behind me. I didn't know what it was, and I wasn't too excited to find out!

It was still daytime, so I didn't think it would be a monster, but to be on the safe side, I really wanted to go back home and climb into my safe, fortified closet.

But my cows and chickens were getting nervous, so I decided to go investigate. After all—whatever bothered my friends, bothers me!

Don't ask why, but for *some* reason, I didn't think I needed anything more than my farm clothes and a tool! Yeah ... sometimes I just don't plan ahead very well...

Anyway ... off I went into the surrounding woods, armed with nothing but a shovel.

I crept around, behind the trees, trying to see what was making noise back there before *it* saw *me*.

A few yards ahead, I heard wild pigs squealing, and I became nervous. The sound of squealing pigs just ... *gets* to me. Tightening my grip around my stone shovel, creeping forward, I tried to peek around the corner...

Suddenly, a stampede of wild chickens and pigs came rushing at me!

"Ahhh! Ahhh!" I yelled, waving my shovel in front of me and closing my eyes.

I was sure that I was going to be trampled by the animals! It was terrifying!

Jumping back behind a tree as quickly as I could, I tried to make myself as small as possible! I felt the animals rush past me. The chicken feathers hit my face as they flew by, and a couple of pigs rammed into my legs, but I refused to move! I wouldn't be pushed out of my hiding place!

I stayed put until I heard the animals retreating far, far behind me, then I looked around me and down at my body.

Still in one piece, somehow! But amidst the chaos of the stampede I lost my shovel!

Great! Now, I had no form of defense.

Oh well, I thought. At least I was alive...

"Well, that was a close one!" I said to no one.

Very slowly, I moved out from behind my safe, solid tree, and looked around. The forest was trampled, and blocks of dirt and grass were scattered everywhere! Puzzled, I looked around for clues.

What were the wild animals running from?

Sometimes, I can be slow to react, and quite distracted. So, as I was looking around, trying to figure out what the animals had been running from, I somehow *completely* overlooked the only thing still moving in the forest!

How?

I have no idea!

While I was looking around and scratching my head like a dummy, that *creature* came at me, approaching *fast!* I suddenly looked up and noticed the mob just a *few feet* away from me, and I panicked!

Yes, yes. I know that you're supposed to remain *calm* in panic situations, but how exactly was I supposed to react when I saw a *creeper* running at me?! It was practically *sprinting!*

It was moving so fast, I swear, that if the creeper had hair, it would have been flapping wildly behind him!

"Oh no!" I cried.

I turned around, trying not to trip over my own feet, and ran back to the village.

All I saw were trees. Which way had I gone?? Dang it!

I tried to run, but didn't get anywhere.

Ooph! Ooph! Ooph!

"Move! Move!" I screamed.

I was stuck on a tree.

Ooph!

"Dumb tree!"

That's right—I crashed into one tree again and again! At the *worst possible* time to be clumsy, I just kept ramming myself into a tree as the creeper darted toward me like green death...

Finally, able to skirt around the ridiculous tree, I ran as fast as I could back to my village. I didn't dare look behind me—I knew he was there. I could almost feel his hissing breath on my back, and I was in such a panic!

Yup, I'm going to die, I thought.

"I am *so* going to die!" I yelled. That was all I kept thinking as I ran.

The village came into view and I hoped that I would make it—that the creeper would somehow *not* blow up before I found some sort of safety.

Looking back on the situation *now*, I don't know why it didn't hit me that he hadn't exploded yet. But honestly, I wasn't really stopping to ponder the questions of the universe when I was running for my life!

My body slammed against the front door of my cabin as I fell onto it, zipped through, and shut the door shut behind me. I stumbled again, because that's just what I *do* when I'm fighting for my life, and I half-stumbled, half-crawled into my closet.

Could my closet withstand the explosion of a creeper? *Who knows?* All I knew was that I had made that closet, my own little 'panic room', as solid as I could, just in case anything bad ever happened.

As I sat, closed up in the small space, panting, waiting for the explosion that I knew would come, I yelled at myself.

"Steve! You should have dug down! Why didn't you dig down?!"

But there was not time to dig.

Oh yeah—and I also lost my shovel!

All I could do now was sit and wait for the explosion, and hope that the creeper didn't blow me up along with my house...

I waited—not sure for how long.

I probably waited longer than what made sense, but *hey*, when you think you're on the brink of death, common sense kind of goes out the window!

Slowly, *very* slowly, I opened the door to my closet.

I peeked around the corner and looked around my room. There was nothing there. No explosion hole, and no creeper. I felt myself begin to breathe again.

Maybe it had left?

On all fours, I crawled out, keeping my body low to the ground. I heard a thump from somewhere and froze. I could have *fainted* from the fear I felt.

The same *thump* sound repeated over and over again, and nothing happened.

Thump. Thump. Thump...

I relaxed a bit. Slowly advancing, I came to the wall that separated the kitchen and the bedroom.

There, lying almost completely on my belly, I looked around the corner.

There was definitely something making that noise, but I couldn't figure out what it was! To my horror, I looked and saw that the *creeper* was running into my door—over and over again!

Thump. Thump. Thump...

Panic seized me and I scrambled back to my closet.

"No good! He's not gone yet!" I cried to myself.

I waited a little longer. Now, I could hear the thudding sound from my safe room. And I began to wonder, *why hadn't the thing blown up?*

Thump. Thump. Thump...

As I waited, the *thumping* sound became almost funny, since all I heard was the sound of the creeper banging into my door, like a brainless robot.

Thump. Thump. Thump...

It really wasn't going away!

After more time passed, not sure how long, I decided to come out again.

The creeper was obviously not going to blow up. I hoped that if he *was* going to blow up, he would have done it by now. Even still—I emerged from the closet *slowly* and with caution.

Thump. Thump. Thump...

Yup. It was still running into my door, alright.

I contemplated opening to the door to the creeper.

"What??" I asked myself. "Why would I do that?"

Time passed.

Thump. Thump. Thump...

"Well," I said, "I guess I'd need to deal with this sooner or later!"

Besides, I didn't want the creeper to blow up my house and a random villager if anyone wandered over here.

Before I opened the door, I sat back down and analyzed the situation.

This had to be handled with *great care* or things could go bad very quickly. I thought a little bit more, and decided upon a plan of action.

I decided that I *would* open the door, and because I was very smart when I wasn't running for my life, I put on my *diamond armor*.

Since I don't fight bad guys, I don't believe I've ever even been *hit* while wearing this armor before. I bet it's really strong. But how useful would it be if the creeper decided to go *boom?*

Well, hopefully he didn't.

I smacked myself in the head.

Hoping that a creeper wouldn't go *boom*?

I blame *loneliness* for muddling my brain...

After checking, double checking, and *triple* checking that my armor was secure and I was good to go, I *very slowly* made my way to the door.

Thump. Thump. Thump...

I crept up next to the thick, wooden door, as if the monster could have seen me through the solid wood of the cabin walls. My knees began to shake a little, but I told myself to calm down.

"You can do this, Steve," I said.

Thump. Thump. Thump...

Okay! Ready??

One . . . two . . . three!

I opened the door.

And in walked the creeper!

"Ah!" I cried and jumped back, slamming my armor up against the wall.

Well, what did I *expect* would happen?

For one thing, I didn't expect him to just walk right in the *millisecond* I opened the door! Not that *fast*, maybe. Yet, here he was, suddenly roaming around my cabin!

My heart beat so fast, I thought it would break right through my diamond armor! I grabbed onto my chest, trying to calm myself when I almost fainted!

The creeper was looking right at me! His big, sad, black eyes were deep and dark.

And he walked straight up to me!

"No!" I cried. "Stay away!" I scrambled backwards, but there was still a wall behind me.

He wasn't listening. He simply kept coming closer, and I closed my eyes. Not the best thing to do—but I panicked!

This is it, I thought. *I am going to die!*

I waited for the *BOOM*—for my house to be blown to smithereens...

"Ahhhh...?"

I cringed.

But I didn't explode. I felt the creeper bump into me and then it walked back and did it again.

Bonk. Bonk...

Its skin was rough and made me think of leaves.

The panic within me started to settle after the third time it ran into me. I was still nervous, don't get me wrong, but I just wasn't on the verge of *fainting* anymore!

I cracked open an eye.

"Uhmmm . . . okay?"

It wasn't blowing up. It wasn't even attacking me. The creeper just kept walking into me over and over again.

Bonk. Bonk. Bonk...

Was it *brain damaged*?

I stepped out of the creeper's way, and it stopped, as if it suddenly realized that it had been colliding into a Minecraftian this entire time.

The creeper looked at me.

"Uh ... hi?"

It took a step back, then moved its head to rub against my arm. I flinched, still not accustomed to the touch of a monster. I reached out slowly, and pet its head, and it seemed to like it!

Yup. Like a really, really thick bush. Leaves. Soft and dense, but a little crinkly.

"Okay. This is weird."

"*Rrrrrrrrrrrr*," it said.

After a while of feeling the creeper's strange skin, I decided to try and ignore it.

Maybe it would go away.

The creeper stared at me with its big, sad, black eyes.

I'll give you a hint. It didn't go away. The green mob followed me around for the rest of the day! I wore my armor, just to be on the safe side, and it hung around.

The creeper was there when I watered my yard, weeded my garden, and tended to my vegetables. It was even there when I put the animals to sleep and gave them their dinner!

The creature's strange face was hard to understand, its dark eyes wide and frowning mouth gaping, but it seemed to be in *awe* of my animals!

It was so funny.

When I went into the animal pen and poured the food for the cows and chickens, the creeper came in after me and decided that it wanted to *pet* the chickens. So there went the creeper, trying to pet the chickens with his weird, little clawed foot. They kept *bawking* and flying away, probably very angry at having their dinner disturbed by a new, large creature trying to touch them.

All I could do was laugh the entire time...

The creeper tripped a few times when the animals startled him, and fell over. The first time the creeper fell down, I almost screamed! But when it didn't explode—again—I went over to the fallen mob and helped it up.

It had better luck with the cows, needless to say. They didn't mind something petting them while they ate.

By the time I went inside for dinner, with the creeper still following me, I was yapping away at it about how life was around the village. The green mob felt like a *new friend*.

I put away my armor, almost embarrassed to think that I needed it in the first place, then I came out into the main room to find the creeper running into the wall again.

Thump. Thump. Thump...

I laughed, and led my guest to the kitchen.

"So what do you want for dinner, huh?"

It didn't answer, but just looked at me.

"Steak and potatoes sounds great to me, too!"

I set out a plate for each of us and, much to my surprise, the creeper ate all of his food! It leaned over and ate without hands, like a dog. I smiled. It had been such a long *time since* I'd had company over for dinner.

After the dishes were put away and it was time for bed, I set up a spot for the green guy to sleep in my closet.

It just didn't feel right to send him outside.

I know, I know! That was still kind of mean! Sleeping in a *closet*, that is.

But I was still afraid at the time that it might still blow up, and I was hoping the fortified walls would protect me.

At first, I thought that the creeper would be mad at me. But as soon as I turned around to check on him, he was asleep on the mat. I smiled. He looked very peaceful, and I shut off the lights.

He? Did I just think of the creeper as a 'he'?

Eh. Whatever. It would be easier.

My bed squeaked under me, and I tried to be as quiet as possible to avoid waking him. That would have been rude. I looked up at the ceiling, and laughed to myself.

What a *really* weird day!

Outside, my chickens clucked and I looked back over at the closet.

Just this morning, I was terrified that a monster would somehow breech my walls. And tonight, I had a *creeper* sleeping under my roof!

Do creepers even sleep? I looked over, but couldn't see his face in the dark.

Life can be so funny!

Pssssst!!
Liking the story? Don't forget to join my Mailing List! I'll send you *free books* and stuff! (www.SkeletonSteve.com)

Day 2

Well, today I just about had a heart attack. Honestly. It was *terrifying!*

I woke up, and forgot that I had let a *creeper* into my house.

So, silly me, I turned over and nearly jumped out of my skin when I saw a creeper standing *right next to me*, watching me sleep.

We both jumped when I screamed.

"Hssssssss!" the creeper exclaimed in surprise.

I think I may have cried a little...

Creepy creeper!

After scaring the green guy and myself to nearly death, I remembered that I had let this mob stay with me last night.

I sat down on my bed, gripping at my heart, wondering if it was still beating and relaxed. The creeper slowly inched toward my bed, obviously startled by my outburst, and hovered around me.

Patting the side of my bed, I motioned for him to sit down.

The monster made a little *hop*, and his angular body squished onto my mattress next to me.

"Man! You almost gave me a *heart attack* there, buddy!" I said.

Petting his blocky, leafy head, I was delighted when he made a happy hissing, purring sound. "You like that?" I laughed.

"*Grrrrrrr*," he said.

Yes, I know that creepers aren't the first thing to come to mind when someone thinks of *making friends*, but this guy felt like a real friend to me! I felt like he was really responding to my affections, and I liked it.

"Well, you wanna eat some breakfast after that *crazy* start to the day?"

He *grrr-ed* some more, and made a bunch of growling, hissing sounds. Was he like an animal? Or was it more like a real language? Did he just try to make a sentence in his own weird creeper language?

I contemplated the creeper's intelligence as I got dressed.

The creeper and I had a hearty breakfast of beef and eggs, and I laughed at how different my life had suddenly become in 24 hours. It was all because I had ventured out of the village to explore yesterday when this creeper happened to be wandering around in the woods.

Life. It was funny that way.

"Ready to do some chores?"

Yeah, I know, most people wouldn't be too excited to do *chores*, and although I didn't mind them myself, I was a little excited to have a friend to help me with them today!

The creeper seemed to nod, and we left the table.

We harvested the wheat and some other crops. The creeper mostly just *kicked* at the leafy greens, but it was nice to have company for a change. I told him all about the different kinds of vegetables I grew, and how to grow them best. I showed him the greenhouse I'd built behind my cabin.

When we went to feed the chickens and the cows today, he tried to pet them *again.* And he fell, *again*! It was honestly the funniest thing I'd ever seen.

I even nudged him a bit and joked with him, as if he would be able to respond. The creeper didn't respond, obviously, but I felt like he understood me, and was laughing at my joke in his own way.

"Come on buddy. Time to go fishing!"

It was clear that this creeper didn't really have any idea about how to fish. But he came along with me anyway, and while we walked, I explained to him the intricacies of fishing poles and boats.

almost *every* sentence I spoke for the next five minutes!

"*Grrrrrrrr,*" Cree said.

"Alright, alright," I said, "I guess I'm annoying you now."

I laughed. I didn't think that the creeper was annoyed *per se*, but I decided to give it a rest, and sighed very deeply with great satisfaction.

I finally had a friend!

And his name was Cree.

We sat out there on the shore for a long time, just watching the water rise and fall. I don't even remember if we even caught fish! All I know is that right when we were about get my things together to go home and do the end-of-the-day chores, everything went terribly wrong!

For some silly reason, I thought it would be a good idea to go out into the water and have a quick swim.

Thinking back to it now, that afternoon swim was a *terrible* idea, but I didn't know it at the time...

So, I was splashing around, happy with my fortunate turn in life, while Cree watched me from the shore, and all of a sudden, I felt something grab me!

Without warning, I was underwater, choking and gasping for air!

I tried as hard as I could to swim up to the surface, but whatever *had me* was pulling me under—deeper and deeper—and was not letting go!

I looked down at my ankle, and to my horror, saw a giant tentacle wrapped around almost my entire leg! It was a giant squid! And it was pulling me down *fast!*

Now, because, as I've mentioned, my common sense goes *right* out the window in a time of panic, so I started shouting and fighting against the squid which was obviously much stronger than me. Plus, since I was screaming and shouting, all of my oxygen was quickly depleted, and I soon realized that I was in *serious* trouble!

I kicked at the tentacle with my free leg, but the squid felt like it was made of rubber and muscles, and didn't seem to care at all. It was just swimming on its own *squidy* way, taking a quick snack with it, down to the ocean depths...

Again all I kept thinking was, *I'm going to die*. I'm dying today, and this was how I was going to go...

Suddenly, something hit the back of my head. I looked up, and, to my amazement, saw that it was Cree!

My creeper buddy had jumped into the water and swam toward me to try and drag me out! Wrapped my arms around his thick, plant-like body, I struggled against the squid, trying for the surface.

Cree pulled and struggled with all his might, moving his four legs as hard as he could, struggling to pull me away from the giant tentacle...

Just when it seemed like we were both going to drown, the squid let go, as if it had lost interest in me, and we *popped* up to the surface!

I gasped for air, and felt the sunlight in my eyes when we broke through.

You can imagine the joy I felt!

Just like that, Cree and I were splashing in the water not far from shore, as if there never was a huge sea monster down below that tried to eat me. Cree didn't stop swimming until he had completely dragged me ashore. I was gasping and choking for air. I had almost drowned!

My lungs tried to gulp down the air I had lost. The sand was wet and rough against my skin. Cree, because he was worried about me, hovered over, peering into my face with his creeper face to make sure that I was alright.

Even though I'm sure Cree meant well, I wasn't thinking straight, and made a terrible mistake. Starved for oxygen and panicked by the creeper almost smothering me with worry, I suddenly felt *desperate* to have some space, and did something I immediately regretted.

Cree was standing over me, trying to nudge me with his head to make sure that I was okay and alive. I feebly pushed him away, gasping for breath, and when he pressed his heavy body in on me again, I kicked him away with all of my might.

"Get off!" I yelled.

Cree's creeper face didn't have many expressions, but I was quickly able to see that I hurt his feelings.

He stared at me for a moment with sad, dark eyes and a gaping frown, then turned and darted away to the trees.

"No, wait!" I cried. "I'm sorry, Cree!"

My new friend looked back for a moment, and I swear I could see hurt and betrayal in his black eyes. My soul ached for him. I had just yelled at him after he saved my life! It was just panicky stuff while I was desperate for fresh air, but *he* didn't understand that.

"Cree! Wait!"

Cree turned around again and bolted for the woods.

He was gone.

I didn't go after him. Not for any good reason, but simply because it didn't occur to me to do so. I don't know why. I mean, usually when you get into a fight with a friend, you want to make up, right? But instead, I lay in the sand, the sun drying the water on my skin and in my clothes.

After a few more minutes of trying to process that I was still alive, I stood, and very slowly made my way back to my cabin.

I waited for Cree, sitting on my bed, hoping he'd come back. I left the door open, and stared out at the sunlit village outside.

When I got tired of sitting, I moved to the kitchen table. But my friend didn't come back. I made some dinner for both of us and set it out, but Cree didn't show up to eat.

A few hours after sunset, I put away the food, and realized that Cree wasn't coming home.

Day 3

I tried to sleep, but it was useless. I was worrying so much about my new friend. Cree was still out there, all alone, because of me. I kept looking out of my windows, hoping to see a creeper walking toward my cabin. Hoping to see Cree walking into my door over and over again.

But as the night crept on, I lost hope.

I waited almost *all night* to see if Cree came back, but he didn't.

I was so afraid that something bad had happened to him. What if a mob of skeletons ambushed him? I teared up at the thought of my friend full of arrows from those vicious monsters.

What if another creeper blew up around him?

As I sat, my imagination running wild, I thought I heard something.

Far away, I thought I heard a *boom*—a creeper exploding, maybe.

I was suddenly choking with panic. That had to be him! Blowing up for some reason! Cree was gone. My best friend was gone!

"Now, just *calm down* Steve!" I told myself. "You don't know that for a fact! You could have just imagined the entire thing!"

Was that an explosion? An exploding creeper? Was it *Cree* exploding? It was a still serious possibility...

In my paranoia, I instantly imagined the worst case scenario, and threw myself into more of a panic.

I tried to tell myself that it was just my crazy imagination, over and over again, to try to calm myself down, but it didn't really work. All I thought about was *Cree*.

Late in the night, close to morning, I decided that I was going to go out and find him. I'd leave at dawn. I was going to go out and explore — do *everything I could* to try and find my friend and bring him home.

No matter what.

The sun wasn't quite out yet when I finished buckling into my armor and stashing all of my adventuring gear. After many failed attempts at sleep, I watched the horizon, waiting for the orange-pink tint of sunrise.

But the sun wasn't coming fast enough for me! It seemed like the entire world wanted to slow down just as I wanted everything to speed up.

Maddening.

"Come on! Come on!" I said to the world outside.

I ended up being too impatient for my own good, and, before it was fully dawn, I ran out of my front door and into the dark, surrounding woods.

Even before I had crossed the thick line of trees, I saw monsters roaming around. They were all trying to find some sort of shelter for the day, and as I sped past them, I became afraid.

Were there usually *this many* monsters out close to the morning? Why so many?

The trees scraped at my armor as I crashed through the branches and bushes, scratching at the diamond shell harmlessly and not touching my skin. I wasn't really going in any particular direction. I wasn't following a path or trying to strategize my plan of attack.

I just ran through the woods, because my friend was out here somewhere, and I had to find him!

Looking back, I realize that I wasn't very quiet. Actually, I was the complete opposite! In my desperation to find Cree, I threw caution to the wind, and was very sloppy ... and very *loud!* It wasn't long before I had attracted a whole lot of hostile attention.

The skeletons were the first to notice. I think, in my rush, I might have even hit one with my armored shoulder as I crashed through the trees. Yes—bad idea, but I didn't know what to do.

I was panicking!

An arrow whistled past me.

"No!" I yelled. "I don't have *time* for this!"

But the skeletons clearly did not care about my goal. They shot arrows at me and I took cover behind a thick tree trunk, hoping that my armor would protect the rest of my body that, especially anywhere exposed.

I looked around and saw that there were thick, hanging vines nearby. Was there a jungle over here? Had I even come *out* this way before? I hardly ever left the village.

If I made it to the vines, I could hide there until the mobs closed the distance, then I could take them by surprise!

"Come on, Steve. Let's do this!"

I sprinted over to back behind the vines, then ducked out of sight until I heard the confused clicking and clattering of the skeletons nearby. The mob archers couldn't really *speak*, but by the sounds of their bones hitting each other, I could tell that they were confused.

Great!

Was I imagining that? No matter—I had the element of surprise!

But then, just when I thought I was in the clear, *more* skeletons came up behind me! I was being surrounded...

"Oh, no..."

This was all my fault!

If I hadn't yelled at Cree, he wouldn't have run away! If I hadn't panicked and acted without thinking, I wouldn't have even gotten into so much trouble—much less surrounded by deadly skeleton archers.

"Okay," I told myself. "You *have* to *deal* with this to find Cree!" And even as I tried to pump myself up, I dreaded knowing what I had to do.

I had to fight them.

All of them.

By myself.

Taking a deep breath and checking my diamond armor, I hefted my shield and readied myself for battle. I looked around and saw that the skeleton squad was breaking through the thick vines. They were not afraid of me, because they had the numbers. I knew that my hiding spot wouldn't be good for much longer.

After deciding which part of the vines would be the easiest to break through, I let out a *battle cry*, and charged at the wall of monsters!

I hacked through vines and bones and kept my shield high. I tried not to pay attention to the arrows whistling through the air. The vines tangled up around me, but I kept moving. Arrows swished past me and *thunked* into my shield as I continued to advance on the monsters. Another skeleton shattered into pieces under my blade.

"Come on!" I cried. "Just a few more!"

There weren't many skeletons in the attack path I chose, thankfully, and as I pushed through them, I could see a break in their formation. I sprinted through, waving my sword around like a maniac trying to knock back as many of them.

I ran for my life.

"Cree! *Cree!*"

Looking back on the situation now, I'm not sure why I was still hoping that I would find him! I guess it was because I was afraid to die, and didn't want to be alone. It also probably had to do with the fact that I wanted someone to hear my shouting and come to my aid.

But there wouldn't be anyone out in this part of the forest just before dawn.

I was alone.

And I wasn't too sure if I was going to make it.

The monsters quickly recovered from my attack, and caught up to me. I could hear all of them changing direction and heading my way. They seemed to have surrounded me again, and it was amazing that I even managed to escape them at first! Now, they were closing in on me from all of my quickly-planned exits...

Why were there so many skeletons together here?

And where were the *other* monsters?

"This is it," I told myself. "This is the end! Help! *Help!*"

I shouted and shouted, trying to make someone appear around me with my cries of desperation. I made a wish in my head that Alex and my Minecraftian friends would just *happen by* right then! But I knew that they were probably just waking up in their house on the other side of the mountain.

There wasn't anybody around. I felt my gut tighten in fear. I put my back up against a tree and raised my shield. Maybe I'd stand a chance of surviving until the sun came out if I at least made sure they couldn't come up behind me.

I'd do what I could.

Suddenly, I saw something out of the corner of my eye. It was green and moving fast. *Very fast.* Another monster—an attacking creeper!

"No! Dang it!" I cried.

Great—just what I needed when skeletons were already shooting at me. A creeper chasing me, too!

I bolted away from the tree through the barrage of arrows to get away. My shield was covered in them!

"No! Don't blow up! *Don't blow up!*" I stammered, the creeper chasing me and closing...

I changed the direction of my running to get away, but the creeper followed. I knew that any second now, it was going to blow up!

Any second now!

My legs ached, and I was slowing down, my armor and shield growing heavy. I was out of energy, but the creeper on my tail seemed to have energy to spare!

I didn't think of bringing food with me!

Not like I had time to eat anything with a creeper and a dozen skeletons chasing me...

My eyes closed, and I let myself go.

This was it.

I was going to be blown up by a creeper. An arrow whistled past my face. I turned to stand my ground, and raised my shield to hopefully take most of the blast. Squinting my eyes, hiding behind shield, I waited for the boom...

But as I stopped, the creeper stopped with me. And when he didn't explode, I looked over my shield in confusion.

What was going on?

When I made eye contact with the creeper, it lunged at me and tackled me to the ground!

"Oooph! Ow! Urgh!"

I struggled—not very effectively—and the creeper and I rolled down a hill together. We fell into the bushes at the bottom, our bodies tumbling down into a ditch covered with very tall grass.

I was out of breath and confused.

The creeper lay on top of me, and I struggled against its weight, but the green guy *would not move*.

"Hey! Get off! Come on!" I shouted.

The monster's entire form crushed onto my face, as if trying to keep me quiet. Its skin was dry and soft, crackly, like dense, compressed leaves.

And that was when I figured it out.

The creeper wasn't blowing up. It wasn't trying to kill me.

I stopped struggling and looked at him.

"Cree?!" I whispered.

He didn't answer but crushed his weight into me, flattening me out on the grass. His leafy body pressed up against my mouth, making it hard to speak.

"Cree!" I cried, muffled.

Yes—I am that stubborn. Looking back now, I shouldn't have been making so much noise when we were being chased by a big group of skeletons! But *hey*, live and learn.

Cree covered me with his green body as the mobs passed by. He was better camouflaged against the grass than my bright and shiny blue armor. Covering me until the last of the monsters went away, and then a long while longer, he didn't let me move until they were long gone.

I didn't mind. I had found my friend again.

And *again*, he had saved my life.

I realized that creepers were definitely smarter than I had previously thought. They're not like beasts.

When the coast was clear, and Cree was convinced the mobs would not return, he stood up on his four little legs, and rubbed his head against my armored shoulder. I tackled him to the ground in a hug.

"Cree! Oh my gosh! I'm *so* sorry! Thank you so much, Cree! I missed you so much, buddy! You saved me! You saved me!"

"*Rrrrrrrrrr...*"

It didn't matter if he understood me or not. I just hugged him, and he let me hug him. We sat in the ditch and avoided any unnecessary fights until the sun had risen fully and burned up any lingering monsters to piles of ash.

"Come on Cree. Let's go home."

We stood and walked back through the trees to the village. In my panic, I had forgotten that I always carry a *map* in my inventory. Cree looked at me as if amused.

"You know what?" I asked him, sarcastically. "In a panic, all of my common sense goes *out the window*, okay? You know that! So, yes—I *did* forget that I had a map!"

Back at the cabin a short while later, I made us both a hearty meal of beef and eggs. Cree hungrily gobbled up the food, and I happily gave him a second serving.

He purred and hissed.

Cree was a very happy creeper.

After breakfast, we lounged around outside a bit. I didn't really feel like working after the sleepless night and crazy morning. So we just fed the cows and chickens, picked a few vegetables, and then just sat and watched the cows *moo* and the chickens *bawk bawk* for the rest of the day...

And that was when everything got a little complicated ... again!

You know, I get into these sticky situations *all the time*, it seems. Not on purpose though!

Dang! All I wanted was a peaceful life!

Cree and I were lounging on some chairs, watching the animals, when I heard a ruckus from afar.

We heard a group of Minecraftians shouting and laughing.

I smiled, and perked up. My friends from the other side of the mountain were here to visit!

I put my hand on the creeper's plant-like shoulder. Well, where a shoulder would have been, anyway...

"Cree!" I exclaimed. "My friends! Look! Come on, you have to meet them!"

Cree stood up with me, and we walked down the street to meet them halfway across the village from my cabin.

It never occurred to me to be nervous at all about approaching a bunch of rough and tumble adventurers with a *creeper* at my side. Cree had saved my life, after all, *twice*, and I was excited for my friends to hear about the great stories we shared!

My friends turned around the corner of the village's blacksmith building, and ran down the street toward me, Alex in the lead.

"Hey guys!" I yelled, waving as Cree and I approached.

I guess they didn't immediately notice the creeper behind me, because Alex, the first to approach, clapped me over the shoulder and greeted me pretty normally.

"Hey Steve!" she said, flicking her red hair through the air. "You've been very quiet lately. We wanted to come over and make sure you were still alive!" she laughed.

"Man! If only you knew!" I said, laughing back at her.

I looked at the rest of the gang, then looked back at Cree, who had stayed behind me for some reason.

"Cree! Come on!" I said, turning back to my fellow Minecraftians again. "Guys, there's someone I want you to meet! I made a new friend."

"A new friend!" Alex asked. "Is it a *turkey?*"

"Haha, Alex," I said. "You're hilarious." I rolled my eyes.

Cree came up beside me, and I was shocked when everyone immediately produced their weapons and raised their shields!

"Whoa, whoa! Hey no! Stop it!" I stammered. "This is my friend! His name is Cree!"

Alex stared at me as if I had grown a second head, and I heard one of the others take in a deep breath.

"Oh boy," she said...

Box Set Book 2:
Diary of Steve
and the Wimpy Creeper 2

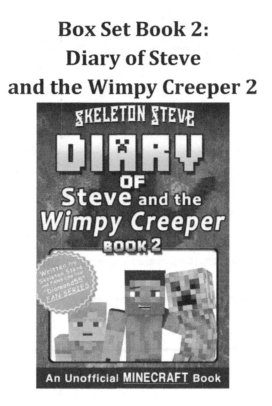

Cree the Creeper ran away!!

After book 1, when Steve introduced his new creeper friend, Cree, to his friends, they scared him away!

Now, Steve is determined to find his new friend and bring him back home. But when the search for Cree leads him into a massive and dangerous underground dungeon, will Steve have the strength and resourcefulness to locate Cree and get out alive?

Day 4

Well, we have some serious problems!

Aaaahhhh!

What crazy stuff I've gotten into since I let a creeper into my home! What ever happened to my easy, simple little life??

Sigh.

Let me start over.

So ... yesterday, Cree, Alex and the gang all *met.*

I was super excited, but when Alex saw him, I realized that maybe this wasn't such a good idea...

My friend became really hostile toward Cree, and it really made me sad to think that my friends wouldn't be able to see past his creeper exterior.

I mean—Cree wasn't just a creeper!

He was my *best friend!*

Alex was really mad at me for endangering myself like this, and she wouldn't lower her weapon even *after* I asked her to. Cree became really *scared*, since he wasn't used to anyone being so threatening towards him, and he *ran away!*

That's right!

My current best friend scared off my *new* best friend! It was a super lousy feeling...

After that, Alex and I got into a really bad argument. It wasn't about her not accepting a *creeper* into our group—it was that she didn't even want to give Cree, my friend, a chance to show her who he was!

It just wasn't *fair!*

She and the other Minecraftians left a after a little while, and I was *very worried* about Cree. The last time he ran off, I went out to get him. This time, I had no idea where he might have gone, because of how scared he was.

"Pfft, he's probably going to the dungeon at the foot of the mountain," Alex had shouted at me before she left.

She did that to upset me.

Alex *knew* that I didn't like dungeons or anything monster-related!

"Whatever!" I shouted back, but part of me knew that she was probably right. My heart dropped at the thought of what I knew I had to do. "Wait! Alex! Where is it?!"

I didn't want to go to a dungeon.

I *really* didn't want to go!

Alex told me how to get there and she seemed to laugh at me, as if she didn't believe that I would take the risk to get out there. One final glance at her, then back at the mountains, and I took a deep breath.

I knew what I had to do.

With my armor ready, weapons on, and super-determined, I traveled to the foot of the mountain over most of the day.

Dungeons are normally pretty small, so the others tell me. They're apparently like a small room with a monster spawner and some treasure. I've never actually seen one.

But, according to Alex, the dungeon in the mountain was 'extra large'—whatever that meant. I guess I was going to see for myself.

"It's alright, man," I told myself. "You know there's a monster spawner. You know what to expect. Be cool. You can handle this..."

There is really no describing how *terrified* I was to go alone on this adventure, but Cree needed me, and I was not going to let him down!

Later in the day, the mountain loomed over me, casting a long and heavy shadow over all of the surrounding foothills. It was enormous! My neck craned all the way back just to try to spy the peak of it, and even still, I couldn't see the very top!

Uh oh! It was getting dark, and fast!

Soon, there would be monsters everywhere! I could already hear the moans and bustling of some zombies stirring awake. In a panic, I ran behind the nearest tree, shaking and hoping that they went away!

As we have established by now, I never make a whole lot of sense when in a *panic* situation. Obviously, hiding behind a tree when there were zombies stumbling around through the forest was *not the best idea!* But for a few seconds, I felt completely safe!

I thought to myself, *you know, Steve, this is actually a bad idea.*

So I looked around for materials to make myself a house. It didn't need to be huge or super-*fortified*, it just needed to hold out the night.

A *hut*, really.

First, I had to strategically plan out my little house.

I wanted to build it somewhere that was as protected as possible to start with. It wasn't going to be very strong, wasn't going to have massive walls or moats or anything, but I knew I could do *something*...

After scouting the area, I decided the best place to build my *hut* was up against the foot of the mountain. This way, the back of my house was against one of the most solid structures in all of creation!

"Good plan, Steve!" I said to myself, "Good plan!"

Zombie footsteps nearby pulled me out of my daydreams.

"Okay!" I said. "Enough planning!"

After scanning my inventory, I decided that I would use my stone tools to dig up some cobblestone, to build a relatively *sturdy* house. Sturdier than *dirt*, anyway.

It was going to be a simple structure, with one room and a door. I also decided not to use any of my diamond gear. There was no sense in wasting them on dirt and rock! I pulled out my backup shovel and pickaxe, made of stone.

I had to work quickly!

The mobs were coming. I could hear the *grrrs* and *hsssssss's* of all the monsters...

Placing cobblestone blocks down, I built a foundation a few stones deep, then built the walls up. I put on a crude roof, a door, plopped a torch onto the wall, and figured I was done.

There. Small, but effective.

I could barely fit into the structure standing, and had to sit to be comfortable, but it was *perfect!* My little hut wouldn't attract too much attention. Hopefully, the monsters would pass it up as they *grrr-ed* and *hssss-ed* their way around the mountain.

The first hour of the night in the hut was the hardest.

Every single noise that came from outside made me nearly jump out of my armor in terror! Every *crack*, *snap*, and *chirp* put me over the edge. I sat with my back against the wall of the mountain, watching the door with an intensity that almost made my head hurt.

"They're right out there! I know it!" I muttered to myself.

Looking back now, I realize that I was being *extremely* paranoid!

You can't blame me, though! It was scary, dark, and there were *tons* of monsters out there! *You* wouldn't have been able to sleep either!

I tried to sleep, but I just couldn't...

About half way through the night I must have passed out, because I was suddenly startled awake by a zombie bashing on my door! My heart almost stopped!

I didn't move—I didn't even breathe!

After a little while, the undead mob seemed to lose interest, and it just walked away.

I didn't sleep *at all* after that.

For the rest of the night, my eyes were completely *glued* to the door, which I knew would be broken down *any minute now*...

Day 5

That 'any minute now' never came, thankfully, and before I knew it, the sun was up and the monsters were all leaving to seek shelter! I was initially extremely happy until it dawned on me that I was right outside of a dungeon.

The odds were pretty good that the monsters from last night all spawned *in* the dungeon and were most likely going *back* into the dungeon for the day!

The dungeon that I was about to go into myself...

"Great. Just great..."

This was not going to be fun for me.

I waited a little longer than I needed to before coming out of my shelter, and looked into the mouth of the cave. A chill ran through my body, and I immediately stiffened in fear. This was *not* going to be the easiest thing in the world.

But I could do it.

I had to.

"You just spent an entire night in a *shack!* You can do this! You can do this, Steve!" I pumped myself up as I paced back and forth outside of the hut. I must have looked like a crazy person.

I jumped in place for a bit to get my energy going, and looked up at the looming mountain again.

"You're not going to scare me! *Cree* is in there! And I'm going for him!"

With my eyes closed and my sword out, I bolted into the den of darkness before I could change my mind!

Immediately, I noticed the change in the air. It was much cooler in here than it was outside. The cave air was also humid, and I could feel the darkness pressing in on me.

A very *creepy-crawly* sort of feeling made me shiver.

I wouldn't stop though! I wasn't going to stop until I was too far in there to chicken out!

I wasn't entirely sure what I was thinking, but for some reason, in my mind, I imagined that the dungeon would just be inside the mouth of the cave. *Let's just walk up to the mountain, step into the dungeon, then step out again! Easy-peasy!*

Thinking ahead to this moment, I never figured that I would have to *look for it* or anything...

So I was a little surprised when I realized that I was going through a maze of stone tunnels, didn't know where I was going, and had no concept of where I would end up!

After a few more minutes of turning left, then right, and *left again*, I stopped, and decided to strategize about how to best accomplish this task.

"Okay!" I said to myself, my voice echoing in the dark, stone cavern. "Let's list out what you came here to do, Steve!

"Goal #1 – Find the dungeon inside the mountain.

Goal #2 – Find Cree and bring him home.

Obstacle #1 — Don't know where the dungeon is.

Obstacle #2 — Lots of monsters."

I nodded to myself to reinforce this. "I can do it!"

The dungeon is at the heart of the caves beneath the mountain. That's what Alex had said...

"If I keep walking, I should be able to find it. I just need to go ... this way?"

What started out as wandering turned into strategized movements into the depths of the stone monster. I figured that if I was going to wander around, I may as well wander into the central depths of the giant structure.

Keep moving forward. Keep moving down.

The tunnels became impossibly dark.

Never in my life had I imagined that there was a level of darkness as intense and as solid as the one that lingered past the end of my torch! Have *you* ever been deep underground?? It's a special kind of dark. Black like you wouldn't believe!

I had to be careful not to use up the torches I brought for the dungeon. So I resisted the temptation to use them to make a path behind me, even though that would have really helped in getting back out.

As I pressed on, the darkness seemed to *slither* out of the way of the light. The shadows looked very slow and almost alive. My skin crawled under my armor out of fear.

The tunnel walls were narrow, not very tall, and I had to slump down sometimes to make it into another passage of the maze.

"I have to be getting there soon," I said, feeling very small.

I had no clue how long I'd been walking those dark and lonely tunnels. It seemed like *forever!*

"Why are there no monsters?" I asked, aloud.

Not that I was *complaining*, but it was strange that I hadn't encountered any mobs this far into the caverns!

There was a very low entrance coming up and it required me to squat down and crawl through the opening. I put my torch away, making sure that I was in the clear before trying to jump. I landed with a loud and heavy *thump* and winced at the how loud it was. The dull sound echoed throughout the maze and immediately attracted something's attention.

I could hear it, moving toward me. Panic began to take over my body, and my shaking hands refused to open up my inventory and take out a torch to at least *see* what it was!

"*Sssss. Rrrrrr,*" something said in the dark.

What kind of monster made *those* noises?!

"Come on! Come on!" I stammered at myself.

"*Mmmmmrrrrrr,*" the creature said, very close to me.

Zombie. It had to be a zombie. I had no way of confirming though, since my torch refused to light!

Suddenly, everything went quiet. My movement stopped. I stood as still as I possibly could, fighting with my body's desire to tremble. Then, without any warning, the sound came again.

"*Rrrrr!*" the zombie said *right next to me.*

"Aaaahhh!" I yelled in surprise.

My armor almost *flew* off of me from how fast I sprinted away. The monster had been right *behind* me!

Behind me?! *Yes!*

Somehow, I had missed an opening somewhere, and the mob had crept up on me from *under* the level I was standing on. I could still hear it behind me, *grrr-ing* and *sssrr-ing*. The more I ran, the further away the sound was.

Stomp, stomp, stomp, stomp!

The heavy armor made my footsteps sound louder and heavier than they normally did. Before I could decide that I didn't need to run anymore, the decision was made for me. Just as I was about to stop, my foot moved into the air, and when it came down to set on the ground, my heart flew out of my chest when I realized that there was absolutely *nothing there!*

"Aaaahhh!" I screamed.

The speed I was running pushed the rest of my body forward and into the empty space. There was nothing to catch me or grab onto.

Only darkness.

I plummeted into the unknown.

"I'm going to die!" I cried.

That's all I was able to yell before I landed on my side, with a crash and the sound of breaking glass...

I must have knocked myself out, because when I awoke later, I couldn't tell which direction I was facing, or where I was! I was waiting for the pain to rise up and tell me that I wouldn't be able to move...

But the pain didn't come.

When nothing happened, I opened my eyes and looked around.

Well, I *tried* to look around. I still couldn't see anything because of how dark the caves were, but I sure was happy to be alive!

Whatever monster was pursuing me in the tunnels above hadn't followed me down. I slowly stood up. I was still surprised that I hadn't *died*. I didn't even break anything!

The tunnel I fell into was bigger than the last one. I couldn't feel any of the walls around me, and after rooting around in my inventory for a while, I lit a torch.

The walls around me, I immediately noticed, were not the raw stone of a natural cave. I reached out to touch them, and realized that they were mossy cobblestone—green and dank with growth.

"Huh ... that's weird," I said to myself. "Most caves don't have moss stone."

A light at the end of the very long tunnel caught my attention.

There was nothing behind me but more wall, and nothing under me or around me of interest. The only opening I could see was the opening with the light, up ahead. I put out my torch and made my way toward the glow.

Creeping up to the opening, I lied low. My belly grazed the surface of the moss stone below me and I *craned* my neck around the corner of the opening to see if the coast was clear. What I saw completely shocked me...

There, right before my eyes, was the dungeon!

It must have been.

The tunnels were *enormous*! So much bigger than the tiny, skinny caverns I was wandering through to get here! There were chains and gates all around. Silverfish slithered away from me. I hadn't even noticed them until now!

My body crashed against the wall as I jumped up and away from the little monsters. Even as small as they were, those silverfish could seriously hurt me! And I didn't have time for that! I needed to find Cree and bring him home!

A sense of relief washed over me when I realized that one goal of my mission had been achieved.

I found the dungeon!

Okay, well, 'found' was maybe a strong word to use. It was more I *fell and stumbled* into the dungeon, but the point of it all was that I was here!

Finally!

"Alright! Good job, Steve!" I said to myself, my voice echoing in the large tunnel. "Good job!"

Yes, I was *extremely* proud of myself. But now that I was here, I didn't really know what to do!

I laughed. I'm not the best planner I guess.

"That's alright! That's alright!" I said to myself. I didn't want to feel like I'd come all this way for nothing! "Plan it out! Gotta *strategize*, Steve, just like last time!"

I heard the moan of a zombie from around a corner, and clamped my hands over my mouth.

I needed to be more quiet! If I tipped off the monsters to my presence, I'd be fighting every mob in here!

So, I thought for a while, then knew what to do.

First, I'd put down some kind of trail of markers—a way to find my way back out. That was why I brought the torches with me!

Then, I would go deep into the dungeon, always following a path to the *right,* until I either found Cree … or a dead end. Then the next tunnel—there were several. Rinse, repeat. I don't know why I chose the *right* tunnel first—it didn't really make any difference, so one was as good as another.

As I crept into the dark, imposing complex, I set up a torch every several steps. Every now and again, I looked back to make sure that my torches weren't being taken down.

By whom? I thought. *Who would take down my torches?* I didn't know—I just wanted to make sure that I didn't have anything following me!

Although the tunnels were enormous, I still felt a little cramped and claustrophobic. It felt like the walls were pressing in on me. The humidity radiating off the moss stone made me sweat as I moved deeper into the dungeon...

Pssssst!!
Liking the story? Don't forget to join my Mailing List! I'll send you *free books* and stuff!
(www.SkeletonSteve.com)

Day 6

I don't know how long I'd been down here, but I kept going. Nothing was going to stop me. I had to find Cree, no matter what!

Not all of the tunnels and passages were lit. Some were, and had torches lining the walls haphazardly, put up randomly and abandoned.

The tunnel I was in right now, however, was dark. There were sections of the path that ended in darkened pods. I *really* didn't want to go in there, afraid that a monster would jump out at me.

But the fact that Cree might be in one of them made me pause.

Argh!

Sometimes, when I was tired, I would go into one of these little pods to rest after making sure that it was clear.

To set up a quick safe place for a nap, first, I would barricade the door with some stone that I still had left over, then I would settle in for a little shuteye.

But I knew that I couldn't stay too long—I'd get caught!

I checked almost every single empty room I passed, just in case. I didn't want to miss the *one* room that Cree could be in.

Sometimes, I heard footsteps and moans inside, so I passed around the occupied rooms and pods with monsters inside as quietly as I could.

After all this time, I was still undetected. *Amazing!*

I was going to have a heart attack down here—I knew it!

For some reason, another room I passed felt a little … different. I couldn't quite put my finger on it, but I listened to my gut and approached more slowly.

I crept up to the entry. First my forehead peaked around the wall, then my eyes and finally my nose.

Immediately, I began to shake. There was something moving in there and it was *huge*. Oh no! Oh no! This was exactly what I was afraid of!

That wasn't Cree.

I knew Cree's shape and size, and this thing was *much* bigger than he was.

My hands began to shake and I held my breath to keep my armor from clattering. My teeth started chattering, so I gulped down the fear in my throat and tried to keep my cool...

In the room ahead of me, a few feet away from my face, was a *giant* spider.

The entire room was covered in enormous, sticky webs. The long strings glistened against the torch light. An enormous spider sat at the very center of the web, waiting for prey to stumble into its clutches.

That prey would have been *me*, if something in my gut hadn't told me to approach with *extreme* caution.

It twitched, turning its head, as if the sound of my armor made it perk up in attention. Its four glowing red eyes scanned the darkness.

My breathing stopped, and I slowly walked away, not once taking my eyes off the entrance to the room, just in case the spider decided to come after me. I could still make a dash for it if the creepy-crawly monster gave chase.

After a few minutes of walking backwards and trying to calm myself, I finally turned around.

Phew! That was a close one!

I could have been eaten by that giant spider, and that would have been that! No home, or Cree, or *anything!*

The end.

I shook my head to clear out the fear that made my brain feel like a fog. Now was not the time for this sort of nonsense.

I kept walking deeper into the dungeon until I finally came upon the monster spawner at the structure's cobblestone heart.

Skeleton bones clanked and clattered in the dark.

Great.

Skeletons. *Eeewgh! Gross!* I *hate* skeletons! No wonder there are so many skeletons around my home!

"On the bright side," I said to myself, "at least you're in the center of the dungeon!"

Next to where I was standing, near the entrance to the monster-spawner room, a chest sat up against the wall. I hoped that there would be something useful inside!

The mobs were far enough away—maybe I could reach the chest without the skeletons noticing!

Creeping over and quietly opening the wooden containers, I found some bones, bread, and rotten flesh. It was practically empty.

Hmmmm. Not the worst, but not the best.

At least there was some bread. I was starving! I hadn't even noticed my hunger until I smelled the old food. I grabbed the loaf, and ate the entire thing there in the dungeon, keeping my eye on the skeletons walking around not far from me.

How had I been so hungry and not noticed it?! Fear is a powerful thing, let me tell you. It really does override all of your other senses!

The monster spawner flashed in the darkness suddenly, and in a puff of smoke, another skeleton appeared near the others.

It occurred to me that this chest with bread and mob junk in it might be the first chest I'd ever opened outside of the village.

What a sheltered life I've lived! I bet if Alex and the others were here, they wouldn't be sneaking around. They'd just kill everything and make the dungeon safe.

As I ate the bread and pondered, I noticed a corridor going off into the darkness near me that was shaped differently than the rest of the dungeon.

How odd. Did my friends carve into the wall there in the past?

After I finished eating the loaf, something in my gut told me that *that* was the way I wanted to go...

I decided to listen to my instincts for a change.

Now, keep in mind, this entire time I'd been putting my torches up on the walls to make sure that I could find my way back. So *la de daa*, there I went putting up my torches willy-nilly, and then I realized with surprise ... there was only one torch left!

"What?!"

My voice echoed through the dark halls.

Out of torches!

I ran back the way I came to take some of my other torches off of the walls, trying to space them out more wisely.

"No! I thought I packed more!"

A skeleton clattered somewhere.

Well, turns out I hadn't. I was going through a monster-infested dungeon, looking for Cree, and now I was almost completely out of torches!

"Great! Just great, Steve!"

I wished I paid more attention up until now, so that I could have divided up the torches better. I had a *whole chest* full of coal back home! But there was nothing I could do about it now.

I looked down the hall. Man, it was *long!*

"Okay, this hall is pretty long ... *but* ... it's probably a dead end!" I whispered to myself. "First, down this hall and then *back*, and you'll have torches again! Brilliant, Steve! Brilliant!"

Slowly, I made my way down the hall.

Knowing that I had only a few torches remaining made me even more afraid of my surroundings, even though the monsters were behind me.

In the pit of my stomach, I felt that this was going to end badly. Somehow, I just *knew* that something bad was going to happen. But I kept going, because *honestly*, in a dark and monster-infested dungeon, things were *already* bad!

I hung my last torch. I wouldn't have enough to make it all the way to the end of the corridor. I'd have to walk the end of it in the dark.

Without a torch to distract me, I wrung my hands together.

"Still hidden," I told myself. "Almost at the end. Almost there, Steve!"

I could almost see the dark outline of the end wall but something in me told me to keep going. *Slower and slower, just a little more,* I thought. Then it turned into ... nope! Turning back!

But I tried to hold out as long as I could. I tried to keep going with my dimming light behind me, barely able to see in the darkness.

By the time I panicked and turned back, I was almost crawling to stay low and avoid being seen by whatever was at the end of this tunnel.

I couldn't do it. I just couldn't. I started back for the last torch I hung on the wall, and felt the guilt hit me.

I had let Cree down.

For some reason, not going to the end of the hallway felt like the worst thing I could have done. It felt like I had just abandoned Cree for some reason, while I crawled back the way I came. This time, however, I didn't crawl away out of fear. I slunk through the corridor, hiding in the shadows and taking back my torches, out of shame. I had just abandoned my best friend to this dungeon! I was a terrible person! In my shame, I paused, and that's when I heard it.

"*Grrrr*," a creature said nearby.

I froze, terrified. What made that sound? I knew I didn't *really* want to know, but I turned around anyway. Why? Because I don't think things through!

As I squinted through the darkness, I could see that there was something down there...

"*Grrrrrrrrr.*"

Yup. There was *definitely* something down there.

"*Grrr.*" Over in the dark. Sounded familiar.

I felt frozen. I saw what it was...

It was a creeper!

"*Grrr,*" it said, and it was on the move.

Coming right at me!

I didn't move. After running away from and running into Cree so many times now, I knew better. I think I learned that not every single creeper was dangerous.

At least, I *hoped* that this was the case!

The approaching creeper might have been Cree!

I really need to give him a necklace or something so I can tell which one he is, I thought to myself.

I shook my head. Why hadn't I thought of that idea sooner? Well, I'd only known Cree for almost a week now, and I don't really prepare too far ahead for bad things to happen!

Mental Note: Prepare for bad things to happen!

Closer and closer the creeper came. Slowly. The mob didn't seem to be in a rush—didn't seem dead set on blowing me up or anything—so I decided that I needed to take a chance.

"Cree?"

If this creeper wasn't Cree, I was in *big* trouble!

It paused and looked at me.

The monster appeared almost completely *black* in the dark, and for one dreadful moment, I didn't think it was Cree. Its sad, black eyes peered at me, looked through me, looked at the hallway behind me...

This was it! I was going to be blown away by a creeper! Again!

Although it was a terrible thing, I didn't feel too bad about how everything was all going to end for me. I had done my very best to find Cree, and if I was going to meet my end like this, I was going to die as a hero!

Not too bad for someone who was afraid of monsters...

I backed away, then fell backwards to the floor. The creeper kept coming, so I began to crawl backwards. Not too fast! I didn't want to trigger an explosion!

The mob paused and looked at me. Oh no! It was going to explode! I don't know why but instead of running away in that pause I just sat there, frozen. It shook its head, then looked at me with more intensity.

This is it!

The creeper jumped at me.

"Aaaaahh!" I screamed.

Thump!

The monster landed on top me and stared down at my pale and horrified face. He didn't explode.

"Cree?!"

I could swear the creeper's frown twisted into a subtle smile...

Day 7

His head rubbed against my helmet and I rolled over, tossing him off my body.

"Cree! It *is* you! Oh my *gosh!* You're alive!"

I hugged him close to me and he *grr-ed* and *hissed* with joy.

"Do you *like* giving me heart attacks?!"

"*Grrrrr. Hisssss!*" he said.

"I'll take that as a yes!" I exclaimed, laughing.

Cree seemed to almost be laughing with me. I couldn't believe I had found him! Actually, *he* had found *me!* What were the odds??

I put my hand where his shoulder would have been and smiled.

"Cree, let's go home!"

We both stood, and were about to go back up the tunnel, back to the monster spawn room, when Cree stood in my way.

"Hey, what's going on?"

He moved backwards, not looking at me as he pushed me backwards with his leafy body—back toward the end of the tunnel.

Oh no. This was bad.

At first, I was very confused, but I knew Cree well enough by now to know that if he was doing this, then it was for a good reason!

As quietly as possible, I darted back to the dead end and made myself as small as I could be. Cree came running behind me and he pushed me into the corner of the room.

He purred at me, as if telling me to stay put.

I nodded, and became a quiet bundle of cloth and armor behind him. Cree stood in front of me, crushing his back against me to try to cover my shiny armor with his green and grassy body.

I heard the clicking before I saw the monster. A skeleton appeared further down the long hallway and looked around, as if trying to find a wayward Minecraftian—a squishy, warm-fleshed Minecraftian who had been shouting and making a ruckus in the tunnel...

Keeping my head down, afraid that if I looked at the skeleton, I would attract his attention, I quietly berated myself for being so loud and dumb!

What was I thinking, causing such commotion in a monster-infested dungeon!? It's a *wonder* I wasn't discovered until now!

The skeleton looked around a little more. Was it trying to decide if he could trust Cree enough to truly be alone in the room?

Cree did not move an inch. He stood tall and protective over me, and I knew that if the skeleton attacked, then Cree would take the full brunt of it to save me.

Please don't attack! Please don't attack! I thought.

I couldn't stand to think that Cree would get hurt trying to save me ... again!

The skeleton archer turned around a few times, as if confused, then walked back down the tunnel. It seemed to have lost interest, but Cree still did not move out from in front of me. He wanted to make sure that the skeleton was really gone before moving.

I didn't budge.

My friend was so much smarter than I had originally thought! Cree really was the *best* friend I could ever ask for.

After Cree was satisfied that the skeleton had gone off on his scary way, he moved and motioned with his head for me to follow him out. I nodded in silence and crept out behind him.

I had learned my lesson! Don't be too loud when there were monsters waiting to get you!

Cree lead the way out of the room and the long hallway, and when he noticed the trail torches I left, he looked up in confusion.

"Oh yeah," I chuckled. "That was me. So we could find our way back out..."

"*Grrrr*," he said.

I wonder what he meant.

Moving over to the lit-up wall, I began taking the torches down, one by one, as we crept along side by side.

At first, everything was going well. The torches were coming down and there wasn't a monster in sight.

Then I heard something and froze...

"Sssh." I said, putting a hand on Cree. "Don't move." I took down the nearest torch and stopped.

My friend must have heard the sound too. Cree had his expressions, as subtle as they were, and I knew that he had heard the sound, too.

There was something behind us.

We moved forward a little more, then stopped.

"Grrrrr. Rrrrr." Cree said.

I looked over at the sound he just made, and realized that Cree wasn't there. He was up ahead just a little.

"Did you say that?" I asked.

Cree shook his head, making a sound like rustling leaves.

Maybe it's all in your head, Steve!

After a few more steps, we paused again.

"Rrrrrgh," something said. It was a deep, rumbly voice.

Not Cree.

Yup. There was *definitely* something behind us!

I began to panic, fumbling with the torches I was still trying to take down. The monster following behind us wasn't just keeping pace—it was faster, and *gaining* on us.

Much faster!

This was bad! This was very bad! A look at Cree, and I think he felt it was really bad too!

"*Grrrrrr!*" Cree said, his dark eyes wide.

"I agree! Run!!"

We both sprinted off as fast as we could!

My armor was loud and noisy. Cree was soft and swift, his clawed little legs almost flying over the moss stone. Man! I needed to become more agile! There was no time for that right now, though! We were being chased! And we had to make it home! I didn't bother to take the rest of the torches, as we rushed down the tunnel. They guided us out of the maze of tunnels and that was *fine by me!* That's all we needed!

Home! We have to make it home!

I listened behind us, trying to hear over the *clank* of my armor and my flying footsteps.

The monster was still coming after us!

Whatever it was, it wasn't going to stop just because of a few torches. I looked at Cree and I felt he might be thinking the same thing.

Neither of us looked back. We focused on the tunnels winding in front of us and trying to see far enough ahead to know which way the torches turned. The last thing we wanted was to have to slow down to *think* about which way to go with this *thing* chasing us.

I started to hear the sounds of other mobs stirring all around us.

We bolted through the monster spawner room, and the skeletons in the room, hanging out around the spawning cage, startled at our explosive entrance.

It gave us a few seconds to get past them before they raised their bows and came after us.

"Grrr. Grrr! Hissss!" Cree exclaimed.

What? I don't know what he was—

I suddenly tripped on the corner of the wooden chest.

Clank! Thunk! Oomph!

I stumbled over myself trying to recover, but managed to keep running. Now was *not* the time! A couple of arrows *thunked* into the cobblestone wall next to my head.

"Aaaahhh!"

We ran past all of the darkened pod rooms.

The giant spider emerged with a ferocious *hissssss*, its long legs stretching out into the hall. I jumped over them and kept going.

"Cree! Keep running!"

The mob behind us sounded bigger and faster than us!

And now it was being joined with everything else in this huge dungeon!

Raaaarrrrr!

And it definitely did not sound very happy. A zombie? No, it was running way too fast for that but I was *not* going to stop to check!

I was getting tired. How long had we been running? This dungeon was a lot bigger than it seemed when I was taking my time through it before.

Finally!

Up ahead I saw the first torch I had put down upon entering the dungeon. We were almost there.

"Cree! We're almost there! Don't stop!"

But Cree was fine. It wasn't Cree that was growing tired—it was me. I felt exhausted at the worst possible time!

No, no, no! The bread was gone, and I had no food!

Again, I had forgotten to bring food on an adventure with me! Not like I could imagine eating on the run, but I would have felt better if I had it, at least!

Looking behind us, into the huge, tall, and wide hall of moss-covered cobblestone, I saw the shadows of monsters stretching in the torchlight from behind us. Grinning skeletons and other shapes, full of elongated claws, weapons, and other pointy bits.

"Gotta make it all the way," I gasped at myself, as I felt my energy dwindling.

I had to make it! I hadn't come this far to stop before I was home!

You can do it! You can do it!

The voice in my head was desperate.

However, even as I told myself this, I saw an obstacle ahead that made my heart lurch.

A wall. A completely solid cobblestone wall.

We both stopped. This could not be the way in. Had we taken a wrong turn somewhere!? No! No! We had followed the torches I had set correctly! I saw them all! Had I messed up somewhere? Oh no!

I could see the torchlight glittering on some broken glass. What was that?

Cree looked back at the group of mobs closing in on us and growled menacingly. There behind us, not far now, was the giant dark form that had been chasing us all this time! It didn't even register to me what it was. The torchlight behind it cast its features into shadows, and all I saw was a huge, scary creature, running at us very, *very* fast!

"Calm down Steve! Calm down!" I shouted at myself.

This was the entrance! I knew that much! Now, we just had to find the *exit*. How had I gotten in?! I looked down at the broken glass again, then my eyes went up to a small hole in the wall, and I remembered how I got in.

I hadn't *walked* in! A monster had chased me and I had *fallen* into the dungeon!

Running over to the broken glass, I saw that it was the remains of a shattered glass vial. There was a piece of paper, still attached to some tiny pieces of glass. It was a label.

I picked it up and looked at it.

"Invisibility"

Alex

What??

One of Alex's Invisibility potions? What's it doing here? Is that what I broke when I fell?

I stuffed the label into my inventory, then looked back to the hole in the wall.

Oh no.

The wall was too tall. We weren't going to be able to make it up. I looked into my inventory again, trying to stay as calm as possible, trying to *not panic,* and to my surprise, I found some meat!

I quickly inhaled the food but did not find any stone or wood or sand. There was nothing I could use make some steps or a ladder. I had used everything I dug up earlier to make the hut.

The monster was just a few paces away. In a few seconds, it would attack us, and we would both die.

Cree hissed and growled at the monster, pushing me into the corner. He was covering me with himself again. My friend was going to defend me, even though it was going to be my fault that we died

I looked down at the ground, sad and disappointed...

No!

It wasn't going to end like this!

Cree and I would fight together! And we would be able to defeat this bizarre monster!

Cree kept shoving me back into the corner and I readied myself for the battle of my life. But just when I was about to draw my sword and turn around, I saw the answer!

There was another opening. Another hole in the wall. But this was a small opening *under* the wall! This was it! This was our way out.

I punched at the floor, trying to break away one more block! Just *one block*, and both Cree and I would be able to fit through it. We would make it! On the other side, I saw a dark void. An unknown hole that would lead us to who-knows-where, but it would be away from the monsters!

Come on! Come on!

Thump! Thump! Thump!

It wasn't breaking, but I kept punching! Nothing was going to stop me now! I had to save us!

Thump! Thump! Crack!

Aha! It was broken!

I turned around, wrapped my arms around Cree and with *all* of my strength, I *yanked* him backwards with me through the hole. I didn't know how long we were going to fall, but any chance falling into darkness was better than no chance fighting against that enormous monster!

We slipped through with a *plop*, and I heard the loud *thud* of the monster smashing into the wall where were just standing.

About six feet below, Cree and I lay frozen stiff in the darkness, both wondering if we had somehow made it...

The cave we fell into was dark. We couldn't see a thing!

The monster roared above us, and scratched at the walls and the hole I made in the floor with its claws. It was too big to get to us, but the other mobs could probably fit through, just like we did.

We had to hurry. Once the monster backed away from the hole, the skeletons and other mobs might move in.

"Don't worry Cree. I've got this," I said.

From out of my dwindling inventory, I pulled one of the handful of torches I recovered before we fled the dungeon.

It didn't light up much of our surroundings, but it was enough to see that we had fallen into a giant underground room of sorts.

Not a cave. A room. Another section of the dungeon?

Pitch black and quiet.

Huh, weird, I thought.

We couldn't stand all the way so we hunched a bit and walked in the direction of the mountain cave's entrance, passing under the tall wall that was previously in our way.

"If we had gotten through that wall," I explained to Cree, "we would have continued this way. So the exit is this way . . . I hope . . ."

I'm not sure how long we walked through the darkness, tunnel after tunnel. The maze seemed *insane*, too crazy to be real. I thought about pulling out my diamond pickaxe to just start making a bee-line through the walls, but as long as the maze kept going in the direction we needed to go, I didn't want to risk breaking through into anything more dangerous.

We were up the creek without a paddle, but we were going to make it through this crazy day!

Night? Day?

To be honest, I wasn't sure what time it was. All I knew was that we needed to get home as soon as possible!

Eventually, the cobblestone stopped, and we were walking through stone cave tunnels once again. It was entirely possible that the tunnel we were in at some point connected with the cave tunnels I had already traveled through before, but it all looked the same, and I couldn't tell.

"There! Look!"

"*Grrrrr!*" Cree said.

Cree looked in the direction my torch was pointing and we both felt overjoyed.

There, just a little ways ahead, were stars.

Night 7

We came out of the caves with grins on our faces. A smile sure looked weird on a creeper's face. Neither of us were sure—was it really over?

Had we *really* just survived through all of that??

Were we really okay?!

Somehow, against the odds, we were here, standing in the cool night air in front of the mountain.

I looked around, trying to orient myself, when I saw ... my shack! It was just on the other side of some trees!

"Cree! Look! My hut! I know how to get home!"

"*Grrrr?*" he asked.

"Yeah ... this was where I stayed the night before I went into the caves! I didn't want to go in during the night," I explained.

ee spun to face me, his expression …
e thwacked my with his head. *Thud!*

"*Grrr!*" he exclaimed. I could only assume he was mad because … maybe because I put myself in danger? He hit me again. And again.

"Ow! Hey! *Stop it!* I had to go get you!" I cried.

Cree lightened up his attacks, and started shoving my shoulder with his head.

"Hey! Come on! Look, we *made* it, so everything is okay! Just don't run off anymore!"

"*Rrrrrr,*" Cree groaned.

"It wasn't all my fault that we're here, you know…" I told him.

Cree slumped down a bit, and stopped pushing. He knew.

"It's alright. We're fine. Just don't do it again," I said, then smiled at him.

"*Rrrrrr.*"

"Now, how do we get home...?"

I paused. Did I hear something?

"Steve!" a voice called out.

"Where are you!?" another yelled.

"What? Cree, did you hear that?" I said, listening to the shout of my name. Somewhere ... over the hill, behind us...

"*Grrrrr*,"Cree said.

Alex! It was Alex and the others! I perked up and shouted back to them.

"Alex! Hey! I'm over here!"

"Steve!" another voice cried. It sounded like Mel, another one of my friends. "Hey guys, he's over here! Alex! He's over here!"

Through the darkness I could see small lights bobbing around and coming our way. I couldn't believe it. There, running toward us in the dark, were my friends! Alex sprinted in front, and I could tell who she was even at this distance from the shape of her armor and her hair.

They closed the distance, and Alex tackled me to the ground.

"You psycho!" she shouted as I tried to throw her off of me. "How could you be so dumb?!"

"Ow! Hey!" I covered myself as she shoved me in anger.

"Did you even think this through, Steve?! What if something happened to you?" she cried.

"*Grrrr!*" Cree growled, and moved to get between us. I stopped him with my hand.

"No, Cree! You're fine!" I said, then turned back to Alex. "Get off me!"

She was sitting on me and had me pinned to the ground, and I tried without success to push her off of me. I was still trying to free myself as Mel and Jack approached.

She punched me in the hip, then climbed off.

"Ow!!" I cried.

She would have probably just punched me in the shoulder, but I was wearing my diamond armor, so she had to find a spot where I was vulnerable. I stood up and dusted myself off as the rest of the gang came around us.

"What are you guys doing here?" I asked. My mind was still racing, and I haven't recovered from the shock that Cree and I had survived the dungeon. And now I was swarmed with my friends out in the middle of nowhere in the middle of the night.

"What do you think?" Alex asked with a huff. "We came out looking for you, dummy! We knew you'd come out this way and when we saw your hut we started looking around. That's when you popped out of the mountain!"

"I was actually here yesterday too," Jack said, sharpening his sword. "I come here every few days to practice fighting. Were there any mobs left?"

What?

"You came looking for me?" I was in total shock.

Is that why the place was so empty?

"Yeah!" Alex was very upset. Even though she's kind of a jerk to me sometimes, I bet she was really worried. "Just because we have a fight over something *dumb* doesn't mean we're not friends anymore! We were going to help you find your friend!"

The rest of the group nodded. She was finally simmering down and relaxing.

"I'm sorry, Alex. I just had to go and get Cree back."

She *humphed* before looking back at me.

"Yeah, I'm sorry too. What a mess we made..."

She walked up to Cree and reached out carefully, petting him on the head. He purred, and leaned into her hand.

"Sorry ... Cree?" she said, trying to remember his name. "We didn't mean to be *jerks* to you! We were just ... surprised! That's all..."

"*Rrrrrrrrrr,*" Cree said.

Alex laughed and smiled suddenly, pulling her hand away. "He feels like dry leaves. So weird!"

Everyone laughed.

"*Grrrr,*" Cree said.

Alex smiled, then turned back to the creeper. "You're not so bad, Cree. Unlike *him!*" She pointed at me.

"Me?!" I said.

"Yeah, don't ever do that again! You had us so worried!"

"I wasn't worried," Jack said.

Alex glared at him.

I turned to the group. "I'm sorry, everyone. Next time, I'll ask you for help."

"We are friends, you know," Mel said. "Friends do stuff *together*."

Everyone nodded, then took turns apologizing to Cree. Cree *grrrrrr-ed* back his acceptance of their apologies, and we all started the walk back to the village.

It was dark and there were monsters out, but I wasn't afraid. Everyone had great armor, and everyone but me held their weapons, and cut down any mobs that came too close. I knew we were safe.

"Alex," I said, catching up to her and rifling through my pack.

"Yeah, Steve?" she said.

I pulled out the paper label from the broken flask. There were still small pieces of glass stuck to it. "What's this?" I asked, and handed it to her.

"Oh, that," she said. "Before I left, I put an invisibility potion in your pack. I figured you might run off and do something brash, so I wanted to make sure you at least had a little help..."

"Invisibility potion??" I asked.

"Yep. Did you like it? Get some good use out of it? I had an extra one, and I don't use those much."

"I don't remember ... um ... in my pack? When I fell through the hole ... I ... as in ..." I broke off into muttering as I remembered the flask breaking under me when I fell into the dungeon in the beginning. Then I snuck past all of those monsters...

My face probably turned pale as I felt a flash of fear, and I realized that I was invisible all the way until ... until I found Cree maybe? I thought about the skeletons, and how I was able to sneak past the monster spawner. I was able to get into that chest without being attacked!

All this time, I thought I was just really good at being sneaky!

Was I invisible the *whole time* I was looking for Cree??

I thought about that huge, scary spider. It was listening to my quiet movements, but didn't see me. And I was so close to it! How did it not see my armored head peeking around the doorway?

Because it was looking right *through* me.

I felt a wash of fear go through me, because I realized that if I didn't accidentally make myself invisible by falling on Alex's potion, I would have probably been gobbled up by monsters.

Jeez.

"Uh … Steve?" Alex asked. She waved a hand in front of my face. "You were saying? The potion…?"

"Um … yeah!" I said, snapping back to reality. "I did. Get use out of it. For sure. Thanks!"

We walked quietly for a while. I listened to Cree's quiet, grassy steps behind me, and the clomping of us Minecraftians in our heavy armor.

"He really is that important to you?" Alex asked. "I still can't believe you went into the mountain *by yourself*, and brought him out with you. Not your style, Steve…"

Alex knew how scared I was of monsters.

"He is, yeah," I responded.

Eventually, we saw the village coming up out of the darkness, and I sighed with relief.

I was home. Finally.

After that crazy adventure, I was home.

"*Grrr*," Cree said, when my house came into view. Did he feel like it was *home* too?

Haha. Correction. *We* were home...

"Thank you all so much for coming to find me and trying to make it right with Cree. It means a lot to me," I told everyone.

"No problem," Mel smiled.

"Put a leash on that thing!" Jack said, then winked. He clapped Cree on the back, and the creeper was jostled, then looked back uncertainly. "Oh, I'm just joshing ya, creeper!" he said, then laughed.

Alex smiled at me. "Steve, you're crazy—you know that?"

I laughed.

Then she got a very dangerous look in her eyes, and I knew that I wasn't going to like it.

"So!" she said. "Since you faced your fears all by yourself, I think it's time you go on an adventure with the rest of us!"

"Yeah! Come on Steve!" Mel said. They all smiled at me.

"What?! Oh, no way!" I said, stammering. "I just got back!" I waved my arms in protest.

"Exactly!" Alex exclaimed. "So rest up, and tomorrow night we go out! That sounds like a plan!"

"But, but ... I've got to take care of—"

"Yeah!" Jack cheered. "Steve coming with us on an adventure!"

"Whoo!" Mel said.

"*Grrrrr!*" Cree exclaimed, trying to smile at the group.

What?! The green, little traitor!

"Cree! No! Really?! You're with *them?!*" I cried.

I couldn't believe Cree!

"Yeah he is!" Alex cheered. "Alright, Cree!" She grinned. "Okay, Steve, so, tomorrow night! It's gonna rock!"

I stood, not knowing what to say, as they all turned to leave, bantering with each other.

"Cree," I said. "Really??"

"*Grrrrrrr,*" he said.

"Oh, and Steve!" Alex called, turning around down the street. "Don't forget your *sword* this time!"

Box Set Book 3:
Diary of Steve
and the Wimpy Creeper 3

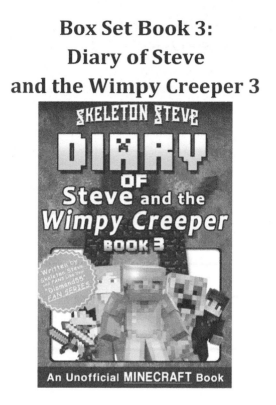

Don't PANIC!!

That's what Steve has told himself for years, but it's never stopped him from losing control in stressful situations!

But now, Steve and Cree the Creeper are heading off with Steve's friends on his first dangerous adventure. And when the toughest warrior of the group is injured, it's up to Steve and Cree to save the day! Will our wimpy hero be able to find his bravery and rescue his friends?

Day 8

Morning.

Morning at my cabin, in my quiet little village.

Normally, I'd be waking up in the sunshine, taking a nice, looooong stretch, and making some breakfast to slowly enjoy before going outside to say hello to my cows and chickens...

Nope! Not today!!

"Okay, do we have it all? Do you think I need more?" I said, looking at Cree, who just looked back at me like I was crazy.

Well! Today was going to be a *big day!*

Like, *super* huge day!

I was going on my first adventure ... somewhere. I hadn't been told yet. But I knew it was going to be *terrible*!

Cree watched me as I packed food and tools and torches and swords and more food and dirt and . . . did I mention food? Yes, food! If it was one thing I had lots of, it was food. And dirt. And cobblestone.

"Food! Cree! We need more food!" I shouted running back to the kitchen. We could *never* have too much of that, I reasoned.

Cree seemed to roll his eyes at me.

I scoffed.

"Hey! Don't look at me like that! You never know what you're gonna need!"

"*Grrrr!*" my creeper pal said back at me.

"Okay, well, when you're totally *starving* and have no food, don't look at me!" I said to him, laughing.

He hissed and snorted, seeming to laugh at me back.

Maybe I was going overboard ... but could you *blame me?!*

It was my first trip out on a *real adventure* and I was so *scared!*

I was not irresponsible, though. I set out plenty of food for my cows and chickens—*more* food and then a little more, just in case!

The cows *mooed* and the chickens *clucked* at me, as if nothing had changed. As if everything in life was going on just as it had been.

I pet my animals, and talked to them, telling them how much they meant to me ... just in case I didn't come back.

It saddened me to think that I might not come back from this. What would happen to them? Would they starve? Maybe the villagers would take care of them...

"*Grrrr!*" Cree said.

"I *know*, Cree! I know! I just want to make sure they're *fed*, that's all!" I said to him.

There were still the crops to tend to before I left. I pet the animals one more time, pat each of their heads again, sadly, then turned away.

"No, you don't get it Cree!" I told him after coming in.

I looked up the sky.

Alex and the others would be coming over the hill soon. Coming over to take me out to the greatest adventure in my life.

"*Okay, Steve, so, Tomorrow night! It's gonna rock!*" Alex had said. "*Don't forget your sword this time!*"

"So much could go wrong," I said to my green friend.

Cree looked at me like I was crazy.

"Seriously, what if I fall into a lava pool?" I asked. "What if Alex *dies?* Or Mel ... or *Jack?!* What if something happens to Jack??"

Don't panic!

Jack was the strongest and fiercest of them. If something happened to *him*, we might as well go home...

"Oh no!" I cried out in a panic. "What if my *armor* breaks?! I should take more armor, huh?"

I *ran* back to my closet and looked over my stuff. I had already packed my diamond armor. "Just in case," I said to myself as I grabbed my other leather and iron armors. "For *backup!*"

Cree followed me into the room.

"*Grrrr!*" he exclaimed.

"You know what, Cree?" I grunted as I crammed the armor into my inventory. "I don't need your *negativity* right now!"

I was beginning to panic. That's what I *did*. It was my *thing*. I looked outside again, and I saw that the sun was going to set soon.

A cold shiver ran through my body and I gulped...

"Well, this is it, guys," I said sadly to my cows and chickens.

I approached for one last petting session.

They looked more bothered than grateful. The chickens *clucked* at me to leave and the cows *mooed* as they lumbered to the other side of the yard. They were tired and wanted to rest. My animals didn't want me to be touching them while they were trying to *sleep!*

"Okay, guys, I'll go, but I *love you guys so much!!*"

I sobbed suddenly.

"Just, you know—just in case I don't make it back!" I shouted back at them as Cree led me away.

Walking up to my cabin, I looked at the door like a was a dead man walking—as if this was the *last time* I would ever come back to my home again. I looked longingly around my kitchen ... my room...

"*Grrr!*" Cree exclaimed, annoyed.

"No, I'm not being dramatic, Cree! I'm just ... preparing for the worst!" I said to him.

With a deep breath, I *threw* myself back and landed on my bed with a soft *thud*.

"This might be the last time I ever lay in my bed again!" I said.

Cree came over and *jumped* onto the bed. He looked down at me with his big, sad eyes, and I could almost hear what he was thinking...

"Yes, yes, I know," I said, shaking my head. "Everything is going to be alright."

Deep down, I hoped that everything would be okay, but *part* of me knew that something could go horribly wrong ... and then that would be ... *bye-bye Steve!*

So long! See ya in the next life! *Hasta la vista, baby!*

After another deep breath, I looked out my window. The sun was setting. The villagers were all running back to their homes, slamming their doors behind them.

I could really relate. They didn't even want to *deal* with the zombies and skeletons that come at night. Why go out looking for trouble??

The time had arrived and I wasn't ready...

Night 8

The villagers were all inside.

Over the hill, I could hear, all too clearly, the mobs rousing from their sleep. The bad guys were coming out, and I was going to be out there with them...

"Oh no," I sighed. With another deep breath, all of sudden, I felt like I'd just died.

Thud! Thud! Thud!

"Ahhhhh! Cree!" I shouted, just about jumping out of my skin.

But Cree was calm. The pounding on the door that had nearly given me a heart attack continued ... then there was shouting.

"Oh no!" I yelled, terrified. "There's a mob outside! Get down, Cree! Hide!"

I ran to my fortified closet and jumped in, just as the door was *broken down!*

Oh no! This was it! This was the end!!

"Hey! Where are you?!" came a voice from outside.

It sounded like Alex.

"Alex!" I whispered to myself in disbelief.

"Hey, Steve! Where are you, man?" Jack cried. I could hear them walking around my house.

My cheeks grew red with embarrassment. I had just been scared into my closet by my friends arriving at my house! How as I *ever* going to make it through the night?

Some adventurer...

"*Grrr!*" Cree said to me.

Cree was outside my closet door. I shook my head at him.

"Is he in there?" Mel asked. I could hear her walking up to the door.

The door cracked open, and I chuckled. "Um ... *hey* guys..." I said.

"What are you doing?" Alex asked. She looked at me with a smirk on her face and a raised eyebrow.

"Um..." I said, covered with my belongings.

Mel helped me up.

Jack shook his head at me.

"Well, um, you see..." I tried to explain. There was a shirt hanging on my raise hand. I threw it behind me.

There really was no good reason for what I had done. The truth of the matter was that I was *scared*. Terrified. I knew it. But I couldn't tell my friends that.

"*Grrr,*" Cree said to them.

"Yeah, we figured," Alex said to Cree, as if she understood him!

"What?!" I asked.

"We know you got *scared!*" Mel said to me.

It was a little embarrassing, truth be told, but there was no reason to deny it...

"It's alright, man," Jack said to me.

For being such a tough guy, he was really understanding. Jack never made me feel like a wimp.

"We know it's your first time going out," he said, smiling, "so don't sweat it! We've got your back."

"Thanks, guys," I said to them, smiling weakly.

They nodded.

"Alright! So! We are going..." Alex said, pausing for dramatic effect...

Everyone smiled at me.

"To the Nether!"

My face must have turned *white* because Mel put her hand on my shoulder.

"Are you okay?" she asked me.

No! I wasn't okay! I was going to the *Nether* ... of all places!

"The *Nether?!*" I shouted.

"Yeah," Alex said. "We need to gather some glowstone for our fortress. So it's a good time to take you out."

The three of them put their things down as if traveling to the deadly Nether wasn't a big deal at all...

"No!" I shouted in protest. "I can't go to *the Nether!* I've never even been out at *night!*"

"Yeah, we know," Jack said, unpacking some stuff. "Which is why we're all going *together*. It's *all* of us. So, you'll be fine!"

"But," I stammered. "How do we even *get* there?!"

"We have to build a portal," Alex said. "So, we brought the stuff. We're going to build it in the center of the village."

She immediately turned to leave the house. The others followed.

"Come on you two," Mel said to Cree and me, looking back over her shoulder. "Setting up the portal is pretty cool to see!"

They all paused to wait for us.

When I didn't move quickly enough, Jack came back and led me out. Cree followed.

"*Come on* Steve," he said. "One foot in front of the other..."

We walked to the center of the village, and they began to construct the portal.

Looking around, I could see the villagers peering out at us from the windows of their houses, their eyes and brows alternating between fear and disapproval.

Jack stood next to me as Alex and Mel put the obsidian blocks together, and tried to advise me about ways to stay safe in the Nether. I heard words like *zombie pigmen* and *fireball* and *bridges* and *mind their own business* ... but I wasn't really listening.

I think I heard him tell me to *stay away from the pigmen* ... something like that. Not too sure, honestly—I was busy panicking in my head about going to the *Nether!*

Cree, on the other hand, looked *super excited*. I tried to feel happy for him, but that didn't stop me from trembling with *fear!*

"*Grrr!*" my creeper pal said in response to whatever Jack was saying.

"Exactly!" Jack said, smiling. "And we'll be right there the whole time!"

The portal was completed sooner than I would have liked, but there was no postponing the inevitable...

Alex cracked a piece of flint and steel just inside the obsidian gateway, and the little spark made the portal come alive with a sickening purple light that swirled and yearned and moaned low and evilly like a thousand zombies waited on the other side.

"Okay!" Alex exclaimed, smiling at the others.

It was time to go.

The portal was dark and evil. I hated it. I hated it standing in the middle of my village. It was *not okay*. The sound that came from it made my skin crawl.

Looking around, I saw the villagers, previously watching from their windows, had disappeared.

They were hiding now.

Legs shaking, I stepped up and into the portal.

Cree stood by me and I held onto him as tightly as I could. His rough, plant-like body gave me the smallest amount of comfort. He didn't seem to mind.

The portal *oogled* and *woogled* and *wiggled*, and I thought I was going to lose my dinner...

But by the time I opened my eyes again, we were somewhere else.

The Nether...

My body stiffened in fear, and Cree had to almost drag me out of the portal.

All I could hear was the loud and weird moan of the portal.

But now, I could hear my friends moving their gear around in the dark, and the crackling of fire in the distance.

"Steve! It's alright, man! We made it!" Jack said suddenly, slapping me on the back.

It was dark. Sort of dark. Hard to explain.

I could still see, but it was dim, like just after the sun goes down.

And everything was dark red.

The ground was ... *squishy*.

"Okay, we gotta get a structure around the portal to keep it safe," Alex said, jumping out. She immediately got to work. "Come on, guys!" she exclaimed. "Right now! Before any ghasts or pigmen appear!"

Even *I* tried to help out. I was shaking, and afraid, but I was going to do my very best!

We built a structure, large enough for the portal and for us to have a little space to sleep and store stuff. I was glad I brought all of this cobblestone and dirt! Of course, I still had a heck of a lot more...

Mel built a single door into the new wall that would lead out into the hellish, scary place. Jack put up some torches, and I could suddenly see much better...

"Alright," I said with a shaky voice. "So what now?"

Mel turned to me and said, "We'll stay here for the night. It's late. Right?"

She turned to Alex.

"Yeah, we should stay here for the night," Alex said.

We all settled in. I lay next to Cree on the weird, squishy ground, and looked through the window in the door. The natural *netherrack* (that's what Jack called it) floor felt like it wasn't sure if it was supposed to be rock or ... meat. I tried to ignore the oily *smell*...

Everything outside the door was *terrifying*! The ghasts made loud noises like weird, demon babies asking for help, and I *swore* I could see pigmen circling our structure.

Eventually, I noticed that everyone was sleeping very soundly.

Me?

I couldn't sleep a *wink!*

Day 9

"Man! That was a great night's rest!" Jack said. "Wouldn't you agree, Steve?"

I glared back at him, my eyes were red with fear and worry.

He knew by my look that I hadn't slept. He just wanted to make fun of me about it...

"*No*, I can't really say the same..." I said.

Everyone laughed.

"Let's *eat up* and get to work!" Alex said.

We opened our packs and began to eat.

"Whoa! Have you got enough food, Steve?!" Mel said to me.

Everyone looked at my inventory and laughed.

"Hey! I just wanted to be prepared," I said, defending myself.

"So what's the plan today?" Jack asked.

"We're gonna explore and gather some glowstone," Alex said. "I doubt we'll have to go far from the structure."

After we finished eating, we made our way out. Jack and Cree stayed with me to make sure I was safe.

Stepping through the door into the open Nether, I can honestly say that the place was *huge* and *terrifying!*

It was unlike anything I had ever seen!

Fire was everywhere!

There were noises coming from all over the place from monsters giant and small alike! It was *insane!*

"Hey! Come on, Steve! Don't drag! We're trying to make it around before we get caught!" Alex called.

Despite the fires all over the place, the *darkness* was immense. I had never seen so much fire and so much darkness all at once!

Aha! I thought. Good thing I packed so many torches!

I started placing them behind me, jamming them into the weird ground.

Torches! Torches! Torches, *everywhere*!

Everywhere we walked, I put a torch! We made a turn, I put two!

I packed *so many* torches!

Not going to lie, I felt very proud of myself.

We finally made it to a spot that Alex and Mel liked, and they began to build towers of dirt to get high up and reach large clusters of glowing rock, hanging from the high, netherrack cave ceilings.

Glowstone...

Jack stayed behind us for a little while to make sure we weren't being followed or ... *hunted.* When nothing came, he, too, built up a tower of dirt and gathered the dust from breaking the glowstone.

Looking around, I saw Cree climbing around on a netherrack cliff. He hopped from red rock to rock ... leapt from squishy stone to stone.

My green friend was having the *time of his life* ... and I smiled. It was great to see him in such a good mood! Seeing him so happy made everything worth it.

"Hey!" Mel called. "Steve!"

"What? What is it?!" I screamed. I panicked. "Are we under *attack?!*"

"No..." she said from atop her dirt column. "I just think that *you* should take advantage of this and get some of your *own* glowstone!"

"Yeah, come on up!" Alex said.

"Yeah, you can *do it!*" Jack exclaimed.

Even Cree growled encouragingly from over on his cliff, flipping and having fun.

"Um, yeah sure ... okay," I said, trying to sound brave.

I didn't want to. I *really* didn't want to.

Honestly, I kind of hoped I could linger around on the ground and just watch the Nether burn. But I wanted to at least *attempt* to have the full experience of this.

Craning my neck, I looked up at the high, dark ceiling, and found a hanging group of glowstone far above me.

Thump.

One block of dirt.

Cool. I could do this. I jumped on top.

I jumped up and placed another block of dirt under my feet before I landed again.

Thump.

Okay. Now, a little higher.

Thump.

Three blocks high. Maybe five or six more, and I could reach the lowest hanging glowing rock.

Thump.

A little higher...

I *jumped* as I suddenly heard the haunting and terrifying call of a ghast, floating around somewhere. Looking up, I could see, through a hole in the cave ceiling leading to another level of this terrible place, a fat, white *horrific* creature passing by, tentacles drifting along under it...

"Nope! Nope!" I shouted.

I jumped off, back down to the squishy ground, putting my small column of dirt between me and the horror that passed by above.

Too much.

A few blocks in, and I *knew* that I couldn't do it...

"Thanks, but I'm fine down here just *watching* you guys!" I said to them.

"Awww, come on," Mel said.

"No, really! Thank you. I'll be fine down here," I said.

They shrugged and kept on collecting.

"Hey, you guys! Look over *there!*" Jack shouted from up on his own dirt tower.

Everyone looked in the direction he was pointing.

"Whoa!" said Mel.

I couldn't see anything from down on the ground. Just more red rock.

"A *Nether fortress!*" Alex said.

Immediately, I knew and regretted that she was excited...

We had been collecting glowstone for a long time by now, and were harvesting more while heading back to the portal when Jack spotted the fortress.

I got a *bad feeling* in the pit of my stomach.

"Tomorrow," Alex said, "we will explore it!"

Mel and Jack let out a *whoop* of joy. I tried not to shake.

"Don't worry, Steve!" Jack said down to me. He must have seen me standing *totally still* down on the ground. Did I *look* scared? "It'll rock!"

Cree *grrr-ed* in excitement and ran to me. He shoved against me in playfulness with his leafy head, and I couldn't help but smile. I really had the best friends ever.

"Well, at least we have a nice, um, *trail* of torches to lead us back to camp!" Alex said.

That was a little jab at me, but I still laughed.

It *was* funny.

There was a snake of torchlight winding through the Nether in front of and behind us, leading out to where we turned around, and going all the way back to our cobblestone structure.

"Yeah, well, least we're not gonna get *lost*," Mel said, smiling.

"Hey! Come on!" I said, laughing. "I just wanted to make sure we got back safe!"

The camp came into view and I sighed.

I had made it through the day...

Day 10

I woke up after another night of little sleep. A few hours after the my friends were all clearly asleep, I stayed away listening to footsteps and pig-like snorting just outside the door.

"Today, we go to the *fortress!*" Alex said over breakfast.

"Yes!" Jack said, pumped. He was *so* excited!

"We can collect a little more glowstone on the way," Mel said.

"Yeah and we can use that time to scope out the fortress," Alex said.

"Steve, what do you think, man?" Jack said to me.

"Yeah, that works," I said, not convinced, staring at my food. With the idea of going into a Nether Fortress hanging over my head, I wasn't all that hungry...

Alex smiled. "It'll be alright," she said to me. "We'll be careful!"

She was right, and I believed her, but I was still scared stiff.

"Cree! Tell Steve it'll all be okay," Mel said.

Cree jumped over and nudged me with his head.

"Grrr!"

"Yes, yes! I know it's gonna be alright," I said laughing.

After breakfast, Mel made a couple of wooden chests, and I watched as all of my friends dumped the glowstone dust they had harvested inside.

"Got anything you want to leave here?" Alex asked me.

"Yeah, you've got like *hundreds* of blocks of cobblestone and several weeks' worth of food and stuff!" Jack said, laughing, gesturing to my bulging pack.

166

I sheepishly shook my head. *No thanks*, I thought. I might need *all* of this stuff!

"Alright, let's go!" Alex cheered.

We traveled along my infinite trail of torches, collecting a little more glowstone along the way.

As we approached the fortress, I began to get nervous. Cree walked near me to comfort me. My imagination ran wild with what a *fortress* in the Nether would look like—I hadn't *seen* it, after all.

Once we went over a hump in the landscape just past where we spotted the fortress yesterday, I gasped as it all came into view...

The Nether opened up into a mind-boggling *huge* cavern. Positively immense. I could see the forms of those horrific ghasts floating around here and there in the distance, and my eyes hurt from the glare of an *ocean* of lava down at the bottom.

Above the lava was a huge, black castle ... multiple castles or *structures* of some kind, all connected by a series of long, skinny black bridges.

It was a city of evil.

Downright *terrifying*.

After some time of approaching along some netherrack cliffs, as I clung closely to Cree for support, Alex stopped when we were close enough to see the entrance of the nearest bridge.

Dark, skeletal forms moved around on it, hard to see in the glare of the lava down below.

"Let's watch and wait for a bit," Alex said.

"Those are *wither skeletons*," Jack whispered to me, pointing at the forms walking around on the bridge.

The wither skeletons were *patrolling* the entrance of the fortress.

"Once they go, we'll slowly make our way in, on that bridge," Alex said.

Everyone nodded.

I looked at the bridge and I gulped. That was a very *long*, scary looking bridge...

Cree pressed up against me and growled. I could do it.

I wouldn't be alone.

Slowly, we approached the *very* long bridge. Honestly, that bridge was *impossibly* long! As we came closer and closer, I could see that it wasn't *black* like I thought, but made of strange, dark reddish-purple bricks.

And it seemed to stretch on for *miles* and *miles!*

"We can take it," Jack said to me. He could sense how nervous I was.

The wither skeletons left, walking back to the main fortress as an organized group.

"Okay! Now!" Alex said.

We made our way across the bridge, weapons drawn, keeping low and attentive. We could do it!

"Something's wrong," Jack whispered to himself.

"What?" Mel asked.

Jack paused. "There's just something not right here—I can *feel it!*"

Alex stopped upon hearing that. She was our leader, but a good leader listened to their most seasoned fighter...

Suddenly, I could hear it.

In a flurry of hissing and bones clattering, a group of wither skeletons *ambushed us!* Their swords were drawn and ready as they stepped out from behind the bridge columns ahead of us. They must have seen us and were waiting for us to pass on the bridge!

Looking behind us, I saw a couple of wither skeletons following our group as well.

We were surrounded!

"Move! Move!" Jack shouted. "Our cover is blown! Let's go!"

He grabbed me and shoved me forward. It looked like my friends were planning to plow ahead through the group of wither skeletons, to fight their way into the fortress instead of going back.

A pair of *ghasts* suddenly swooped in from above to join in the attack.

This was the first time I had ever seen a ghast up close, and I knew I would try to forget...

"Let's go! Let's go!" Alex shouted.

Mel joined her and, they ran forward into the squad of Nether undead.

"Jack! Stay with Steve!" Alex shouted back at him.

Jack hesitated. I knew that he wanted to fight, but he probably knew that I couldn't handle this on my own. He pulled Cree and me behind him, but it was no good.

The ghasts launched fireballs at our group.

One of the fireballs hit the bridge behind Alex and Mel, blowing them off of their feet and into the waiting group of wither skeletons...

The other fireball *exploded* next to Jack, Cree, and me, and we were *blown right off* the bridge!

"*Ahhhhhh!*" Jack and I shouted, as we became airborne, then plummeted off of the side.

"Steve!" Alex shouted.

"Jack!" Mel screamed.

Fortunately, we didn't fall all the way down.

And we didn't fall to our fiery deaths into lava.

Our bodies bounced off a steep netherrack hill below the bridge, and we began to tumble down a steep incline toward the lava shore far below.

Better than falling straight into the burning inferno?

Yes.

Is it *that* much better?

Not really...

"Oooph! Uph!"

I grunted and cried out as every part of my body collided with the netherrack down, down, down the steep hill. It was a good thing I was wearing diamond armor. The ground didn't feel so *squishy* now...

After what felt like falling and tumbling *forever*, we finally stopped and hit some sort of solid ground at the bottom.

We were a little separated, and I could hear Jack groan from his distant landing place.

I saw that Cree ended up near Jack, and was rolling around trying to stand. Eventually, he got to his feet. I couldn't tell how hurt he was.

Both of my friends were moving, hobbling to their feet, and I could also see that both were hurt. I closed my eyes.

I figured that I'd just ... lay here for a while...

Pigmen snorted and stomped around nearby.

I listened to the crackling of the fires around me, and the bubbling of the lava not too far away.

The bridge looked *so high* up there!

"Steve! *Get up!*" a voice called from a distance.

Jack.

Or was it my imagination?

Close by, I heard some noise, and raised my head.

What was that?

I flipped over to my hands and knees, and got low, trying to make myself as small as possible. Something was moving and I *knew* that I didn't want it seeing me.

A group of pigmen appeared around me and I froze...

No! Not now!

They weren't *completely* in the way.

If I moved quietly enough, I pass move through them without making too much a fuss...

Okay, Steve, I told myself. Don't aggravate them. Just *sneak* around them!

Slowly, I moved around and through their group. They stared at me with weird pig eyes and rotting faces. The golden swords then held caught my eye and made me very nervous. A few of the strange, Nether zombies pushed into me, but I was able to avoid a confrontation.

"Good! Good!" I said to myself. "Let's get to Jack and Cree!"

I ran toward my friends, who were composing themselves from the fall, and I stopped to look up. Waaaaay up...

What had happened to Alex and Mel?

After searching for them for a few seconds, my heart sank when I found them. I saw Alex and Mel far above, their armor glimmering in the glow of the lava.

They were being lead into the fortress by the group of wither skeletons!

Oh no!

Captured!

"Gotta get to Jack! Gotta get to Jack!" I repeated to myself as I ran.

I bumped square into a zombie pigman.

Eep! I gasped, and raised my hands to my face.

It squealed, looking back at me with its weird, animal eyes.

"Sorry!!" I cried.

The pigman turned away and wandered off to its tribe.

Jack and Cree were hobbling across the cliff face toward me when I saw them. Jack was scanning the bridge far above us.

"Jack! Cree!"

Jack immediately turned with his sword drawn.

"*Steve!* Man, am I glad to see you!"

I caught up to them and told them immediately what had happened to Mel and Alex.

"You saw them? For sure?" Jack asked.

I nodded.

"Well we gotta go back for them!" Jack said.

I nodded again.

Of course we did.

Did we?

I shook my head. Of course we did!!

Suddenly, Jack turned again, sword drawn, as we were being charged by a several wither skeletons! They had *somehow* followed us down!

"Get behind me!" Jack ordered. Cree and I obeyed.

Jack was a fierce fighter. I knew he could do it, he could beat them—but he *had* just fallen down a big cliff...

The tall, black skeletons collided with Jack, and my warrior friend fought them with everything he had.

Feeling that *panicky feeling* coming on, I decided that I needed to help. I *had* to help!

Let's go! You can do it, Steve! I told myself.

I braced myself, pulled my sword, and *bolted!*

"I can help!" I shouted.

Jack had three wither skeletons on him, and another one or two were coming up behind them.

Holy cow!

I hit a skeleton over the head, and it stumbled. I tried again, but it dodged.

They were *fast!*

"Don't get scared!" I told myself. "You can do this!"

Beside me, I could hear Jack grunting and shouting as he battled it out with the other two skeletons. I only had to deal with one. I could do this!

At first, I thought everything was going well...

But then I panicked and things went *wrong!*

Somehow, a zombie pigman had drifted over to us, probably to see what all the commotion was. In the chaos, I accidentally *wacked* the creature, it squealed in pain, and the world around us *exploded* with violence!

The zombie pigman I hit was suddenly furious, and *attacked!*

I tried to hold it off, while trying to beat at the wither skeleton too! Suddenly, we were *surrounded* by pigmen! They were *everywhere!*

"Oh no!" I cried, my brain freaking out, my heart pounding. "I can't do this!"

I looked to Jack, who was being overwhelmed now by the two wither skeletons and a *swarm* of zombie pigmen. To see him struggling and losing was *too much* for me!

Without a second thought, I *bolted* away from the swarm, leaving Jack by himself.

Cree's big, black eyes went wide. He quickly looked back and forth between me and Jack, then quickly followed me on his four, little legs.

We ran for a small cave.

The swarm was moving. I could tell that Jack was trying to follow us, but it wasn't looking good. Slowly, some of the pigmen around the edges of the group seemed to be losing interest. They wandered back to where they were before joining the attack.

The wither skeletons were gone, but Jack was still surrounded by gold swords and pig zombies...

The closer he came to us, the less and less I saw, pink and green bodies circling my warrior friend, the air filled with the sounds of swords on armor and the grunting and squealing of pigs.

Jack suddenly burst into the cave, beating back a zombie pigman that followed.

"Dirt!" he yelled. "Cover!"

The zombie pigman was on him again. Another pigman pushed through into the cave.

"Now, Steve! Come on!! Help me!"

I felt numb with fear watching, clutching at Cree, but somehow managed to rouse myself into action. Pulling out some dirt blocks, I tried to block up the entrance to the cave as Jack pushed the pigmen back.

By the time the last block was in place, and the pigmen were all grunting and squealing and beating on the other side of the wall, I was suddenly aware that Jack was by himself again, and in *bad* shape.

"Jack!" I shouted.

"Darn it, Steve..." he coughed. "The ... pig ..."

He collapsed to the floor with a *clang*, dropping his sword.

I helped Jack further into the cave, and put down a single torch so that we could see.

Laying Jack down, I knew that I had made a terrible mistake.

Day 11

Jack didn't wake up until the next day.

Even then, he hardly spoke to me. He spent a lot of time in silence, trying to eat and repair his gear.

I couldn't blame him for being sore with me in the least, but that didn't mean I was happy about it.

"Move us further into the cave," he said to me.

I moved him and made a new barricade behind us. I didn't want monsters following us.

Jack fell asleep again for a while.

When I went back to him later, he was awake.

"Jack?" I said to him.

He refused to look at me.

"I'm sorry I left you. I panicked," I said to him, my voice miserable. It was a lousy excuse, but it was all I had.

"It's *not* okay," Jack said staring at the netherrack wall.

I nodded.

"That was dumb and reckless," he said, "but I forgive you."

He took a deep breath and looked at me for the first time since the incident. I could see that he was still badly hurt, but he had forgiven me. That was something at least...

"We have to get Mel and Alex *out* of there," he said looking at my burning torch.

I nodded.

"What should we do?" I asked him.

"I'm thinking..." Jack said.

Cree sat near him to keep him company as I made our cave more hospitable. As the day dragged on, Jack regained *some* of his strength. By that, I mean that he wasn't on the *brink of death* anymore.

But he still wasn't right. The warrior was mostly helpless...

"This is going to count on you *completely*," Jack said, when I sat down with him later.

I gulped and calmed my shaking knees.

Jack had devised a plan, and I played a *big part* in it.

My nerves shot through the roof! Nothing I had ever done before was as important as getting this right. I knew that. Jack couldn't just rescue Alex and Mel himself, because of *me*.

It was *my fault*, and I'd have to fix it.

He was counting on *me!* To have someone so strong and powerful count on me meant a lot, and was determined not to fail him ... again.

"What's the plan?" I asked. "I can do it."

I would not let him down. Even if it killed me.

He nodded. "How much supplies to we have?" he asked me.

Cree looked at me right then, and I kind of *laughed*. The creeper hissed and snorted as he sat on the netherrack. "What gear *don't* we have!" I laughed.

I pulled open my inventory, and Jack's jaw dropped.

"What *didn't* you bring?!" he said. "The kitchen sink?!"

He was amazed at all of the stuff I brought with me. I had pickaxe after pickaxe, two extra sets of armor, food and torches—stacks upon stacks of dirt and stone.

I had *everything* we could possibly need to survive.

"Man, I am *so* glad you overkilled this. This is great! We'll get them out! Believe me!" he said, grinning through his bruises.

And I did believe him.

"The plan," he said, "is simple. We are going to sneak into the fortress, find Mel and Alex, and then all get the heck out of here, back to our world."

He pointed at the pickaxes I brought with me.

"We'll tunnel into the fortress," he said. "You have enough gear for that. Then we need to build a bridge of our own to get *out* of the fortress."

I stayed quiet the entire time Jack spoke. I was in awe at his strategizing. Without him, we would be done for. I would have died, and *none* of us would have made it back home.

"Does that sound good?" he asked me.

I nodded at him and said, "Yes, I can do it. Whatever you say, Jack. I won't let you down."

The warrior grunted in pain and put his hand on my shoulder. "We need to work together—all of us. Even Cree," he said looking at my friend.

"*Grrrrr,*" Cree responded.

"When should we start?" I asked.

Jack thought a bit. "Tomorrow." He looked around the small, dark cave. "For now, let's try to find the perfect place to start digging..."

I built a small gurney to drag Jack around on.

We weren't going to get anywhere without him. I tied the straps of the makeshift bed to Cree, and we were off!

Jack laughed.

"This is almost a bed, Steve," Jack said. "Be careful not to make it any more like a bed..."

"Why not?" I asked.

"Because beds *explode* in the Nether," he replied.

After digging through and scouring the inside of the hill we found a perfect spot. Thankfully, we had already crossed the expanse of lava before we fell off of the bridge. The hill we fell down was just below the fortress's exterior. We wouldn't have to cross the lava to get there.

But we *would* have to cross the lava to get back...

"Start here," Jack indicated. "Dig up this way, then up."

He drew on the floor with a broken piece of stone, indicating a zig zag pattern.

"It'll be like stairs," he said. "That way, we can all get up there. Once we break out, we'll build a *secret* bridge from here," he drew on the ground, "...to *here*. We'll cross that bridge after we free the girls."

I nodded and looked around the cave. How could he tell where we were? I had no idea—it all looked the same to me.

"We should rest for the night," Jack said. "Tomorrow is a new day."

He relaxed in his gurney, and closed his eyes.

But I couldn't rest.

All of this was my fault.

I wasn't going to *stop* until we got out of here...

I took a torch, went to the spot Jack had marked, and began chiseling away.

Day 12

"Grrr!"

"No, I *don't* know Cree!" I said to my green pal as I constructed the bridge. Looking back now, I wasn't sure if I ever actually *understood* him, or if I was just really *that* delusional.

It was no secret: I was *exhausted!*

I don't know what kept me going, but I kept at it. I kept at it even when my body began to shake. The sooner I got this done, the sooner we would save Alex and Mel!

I didn't get too far along in my progress ... I think I kept falling asleep on my pickaxe, but it was more than nothing!

Jack didn't look or feel too great the next day, and although he tried to help me, I was the one doing most of the work.

And I was fine with that! Really I was!

I mean, it was *my* fault that he was injured in the *first* place, but that only meant that I couldn't pay attention to how tired I was...

We ... I ... dug through the fortress wall, just like Jack had planned. He really was one of the greatest strategists *ever!* One thing I *had* accomplished in the night was the secret bridge up to the fortress wall. I figured that laying down my *immense* amount of dirt would be easier than tunneling in through the netherrack.

And I turned out to be right, thankfully.

Now that Jack was awake, it was much easier to work *together* with him, even if he didn't actually *do* much, than to do it alone. Yes, if I was up here, hiding out in the open to build up this dirt bridge to the fortress wall, I would have been alone without Jack. I was *not* going to be an even *worse* friend to Cree by making him stay up with me just to keep my company in this dangerous place...

It wasn't *his* fault we were in this jam!

It was *mine*!

And I was going to do my very best to fix it!

192

Once I finally cut through those dark red blocks and broke into the huge building, Jack in tow and Cree behind me, we snuck through the outer wall.

When we were inside, Jack left the gurney behind, and tried his best to move on his feet.

He was seriously wounded. There was no way he'd be able to fight.

Everything would be resting on my shoulders.

I'd have to be very careful to follow Jack's directions *to the letter.*

"They're probably being held either in the center of the building or in a dungeon of some sort," Jack said, whispering to Cree and me as he moved slowly beside me, using one of my pickaxes to help him walk.

I paid attention to *every single* word he said.

If I didn't focus, I would panic, and panicking would *not* be helpful at the moment! I *refused* to panic! Every time I panicked, it seemed, *bad things* happen!

"What do you want me to do?" I asked, helping him along.

Jack was still limping a little and moved much slower than Cree or me.

To move with any stealth, Jack needed a lot of help, since his armor and weapons were now much *heavier* for him.

Suddenly, from around the corner, I heard something! Jack perked up—he heard it too.

A monster was coming! Bones clattered.

Monsters! *More than one!*

Jack quickly motioned for us to hide behind a jagged staircase, and we *crammed* behind the dark, red stone.

The Nether mobs hissed and made noises at each other in their weird language as they passed.

I held my breath until I was sure that the wither skeletons were gone. I was *not* going to risk getting caught because I *breathed* too loudly...

My hands were closed around my sword's hilt so hard that I thought they would *fall off!* This was unlike anything I had ever experienced before in my life!

"Hey," Jack whispered to me. There was a weak and tired smile on his face. "You're doing *great*, Steve. Stay sharp..."

"Uh, thanks," I said bashfully. I really *was* trying my best!

"Come on! Let's keep moving—we can't stop now! Something tells me they're *near*," Jack said, nodding.

This guy was just naturally *awesome*. I was starting to look at him like my *hero*. Before, I never really got to know him. But Jack was a lot smarter than I thought, and very experienced and clever— and an amazing warrior! I couldn't even begin to *imagine* what being that awesome all the time felt like!

We lurked around that level for a while, before finding a staircase going down into more darkness. We descended to the lower level, and slipped through the shadowy corridors until Cree made a sudden discovery...

My creeper chum leaned against something on the wall, and a door popped open down the hall. It was a *loud* sound in this dim, quiet world of fire and paint—*too* loud, but it was a good thing that we found it.

"What's that?" Jack asked, looking at the button in the wall behind Cree.

"It opened a door!" I said.

"Jack? Steve?" a voice cried from through the doorway. "Is that you??"

It was Alex's voice.

"Jack??" Mel cried from the same place.

We ran to the doorway, Jack hobbling along behind us.

Looking through the doorway, I saw a large room with multiple *jail cells* built into the walls.

196

Each cell, protected by iron bars, held nothing but bones—except one...

"Alex! Mel!" I shouted. "They're here!" I cried back at Jack, who was coming up behind me. "They're in here!"

"*Grrrrrrrr!*" said Cree.

The girls both ran to the iron bars and smiled.

Immediately after, though, Alex's face became dead serious, and I heard the clatter of wither skeletons approaching down the hall. We all scrambled inside the jail room.

"Hide! They'll be coming to check on us!" she hissed at us.

The three of us scanned the room. There weren't many places to hide. In one corner of the room, there was a desk with a chest on top. I could see the girls' gear—armor, swords, and other items—stacked up near the area, too.

We scrambled to the storage area, Jack limping quickly, grunting in pain as he dropped down to hide behind the desk. I hid as best I could, but I knew it wouldn't be long before I was spotted.

"Jack! Are you okay?" Mel asked with great concern when she saw his wounded movements.

And ... Cree! Where was he going to hide??

Jack looked at me and I knew what he was saying. It was *his* turn to hide and *my* time to fight.

"He'll be fine," I assured her. I wasn't sure of it, but there was no point in scaring them now, right?

"We're in a tight spot, Steve," Jack said.

"What are we going to do??" I asked. "There's nowhere for Cree and I to hide!"

"You're going to have to fight them!" Jack said. "Hold them off at the door so you can deal with them one at a time! I'll try to figure something out..."

The wither skeletons approached the doorway, talking in hisses to each other. Indoors, I was surprised by how *tall* they were! I wanted to run, but I stood my ground. *Nothing* was going to shake me! There wasn't anywhere to run to now, anyway...

Next to me, Cree readied himself to attack also and I smiled. I was never alone with Cree at my side.

A chilling calmness settled over me and everything seemed to go quiet as the skeletons stepped inside. The shaking in my knees grew still. My pounding heartbeat, trying to force me into panic mode ... steadied.

When the the first wither skeleton stepped inside, I was pumping myself up to charge, when Cree suddenly pushed back at me with his head. *Stay here*, he seemed to say.

So I did.

As the skeletons walked into the room, inspecting the door—they must have been wondering why it was open—a single creeper ran up to them.

They seemed shocked at seeing an Overworld mob standing in their fortress.

At first, I was horrified at the idea that Cree was about to sacrifice himself for us—that he would blow himself up to kill the wither skeletons and save us all.

My heart and stomach turned cold at the sudden idea.

But that didn't happen.

Instead, Cree walked up to the Nether mobs, craning his head back to talk to the tall undead creatures, and said something to them in their hissing, growling language.

What?!

My eyes widened as I watched from my lousy hiding place, my hands clenching my sword. I was ready to jump in the second things went bad...

The wither skeletons seemed confused, and spoke back to Cree. The group of them went back and forth with my green buddy a few times, speaking in a very similar series of growls and *Rrrrrrrr's* that I'd gotten used to hearing from my friend.

But ... whatever it was Cree had said ... it worked!

All but one of the wither skeletons suddenly drew their swords, turned, and ran back the way they came, clattering off into the distance down the hall.

The remaining wither skeleton drew his sword and moved to guard the prisoners...

It worked! Amazing!

Cree had somehow convinced them to go off chasing something or other down the hall, and a group of *six*, or however many mobs there were, were now down to *one*...

But there was still one to deal with.

I had to fight the last one...

Resisting all of my natural impulses to panic, I gripped my sword tightly, and stepped out to face him.

The wither skeleton's head snapped to look at me, surprised that I was there. It stepped away from the bars of Alex's and Mel's cell, and whirled its long, dark blade in its boney hand.

Cree stayed behind the skeleton, forgotten...

My opponent and I waited for what seemed like *forever* before the it charged at me, its black mouth open in an ugly *hiss*.

Our blades *crashed* together, and the sound scared me.

The wither withdrew and made another blow ... and another!

The swings of its sword came faster and faster!

I tried my best to parry his blows, with my extremely *limited* combat skills. Some attacks hit my blade, some hit my armor. I would have been *dead* without my diamond armor. But I was being backed into a corner!

The wither skeleton towered over me, black-boned and terrifying...

Suddenly, Cree hit him with his head! He threw his body at the wither skeleton, and the skeleton stumbled to the side!

Yeah! We were the dynamic duo! We could do anything!

With Cree helping, I *attacked!*

Swinging my iron blade, I sunk my sword into the skeleton's side with a satisfying *thunk.*

"Yeah!" I heard Alex say. "Get'em, Steve!!"

The long-limbed skeleton came at me again, swinging its sword with frightening skill. I tried to dodge and parry, and took several hits to my diamond armor. My armor was getting beat up but I couldn't care less! As long as it held out!

Cree head-butted the creature again, but it was ready, and didn't lose its balance.

The skeletons in the Nether were *much tougher* than the skeletons back on my world! Bigger, stronger, meaner, uglier...

As the wither skeleton withdrew, circling, swinging its blade as it was probably thinking about how to finish us off, I saw Jack sneaking past behind the battle to the door of Alex and Mel's cell.

My fearsome opponent suddenly swung his sword, and I saw it coming right at my head, when Cree smashed his body into the skeleton's side, throwing off the attack.

The wither skeleton's sword cut into the brick wall with a *clang*, throwing sparks and pieces of stone.

Trying desperately to dodge out of the way, I fell onto my back.

"Oomph!"

The wither was on me in a second, standing tall over me, getting ready to deliver a killing blow...

Cree smashed into the monster again, and the skeleton threw my creeper pal off and to the side with a mighty push. Cree fell to the floor.

As the wither skeleton raised its long, black blade into the air, I held my sword above me, determined to parry the death-dealing attack...

And then the monster hissed in pain, as it broke into pieces under the attack of Alex's and Mel's swords! It turned, surprised, and then with a flash of Alex's blade, its skull popped up into the air, and its body collapsed onto me, a pile of black bones...

The wither skeleton's head fell, bounced on the stone floor, and rolled to a stop, glaring at me.

I guess Jack had gotten them out of the cell after all.

They had just enough time to get their swords and save my life...

With that, the battle was over. Alex helped me to my feet, and Mel helped Cree get to his.

We all beamed at each other, tired and hungry. But we couldn't celebrate—not yet!

We still had to make it *out* of the fortress!

Mel helped Jack as I led the way back to the secret bridge I built the night before.

I didn't dare look back as we escaped through the shadows. It was too scary. I'm sure we *all* wanted to be a safe enough distance before we faced the terrible fortress again...

Finally, Alex was the first to look back, as we climbed the netherrack hill and stood next to my trail of torches again.

She smiled, proud.

"You did great, Steve," she said, patting me on the back. "You too, Cree!"

When I finally turned around, I couldn't *believe* that we had just come out that vast, black, and evil-looking place!

As we took our time traveling back to the portal, we came by some more glowstone.

"Wait," Jack said.

We all stopped.

"Steve, you have to gather some glowstone. Come on, man, after *all that*—you just *gotta!*" he said.

The others nodded.

"*Grrrrr*," Cree said.

I smiled at them and nodded.

Building myself up on a skinny column of dirt, I looked down at my friends standing below me, and with my pickaxe, I harvested my very first cluster of glowstone.

"*Now*," Mel said, "we can go home..."

The trip back wasn't as scary as the trip going *to* the Nether.

I felt like a totally different person after all the terrors I had faced there.

Passing through the portal wasn't scary at all this time. The Nether and the inside of our little structure warped and *oogled* and *woogled* and *wiggled* all around me.

I went through with my eyes open, with Cree at my side.

Then, we were standing in the middle of the village again, with the sky and houses and cobblestone streets warping and blurring around me, until everything quieted down, and we were back in town again...

Cree and I stepped down from the portal onto solid ground.

After some tired goodbyes, Mel, Alex, and Jack turned to leave, and Cree and I made our way back to our quiet little cabin.

Opening my familiar wooden door, before I could convince myself to *clean* something, Cree and I collapsed into the bed...

Day 13

Well! The animals survived!

By the time I got back, my cows and chickens were *starving*!

And they complained about it, let me tell you...

"You guys miss me?" I asked them after breakfast.

The cows *mooed* and the chickens *clucked* but I knew the truth—they only missed their food.

Mooo!

"Whatever!" I shouted. "You guys are liars!" I said to them as I gave them fresh food.

Cree watched me as I changed their drinking water and tended to my crops.

"Well, Cree! What do you wanna do today?" I asked him, wiping the sweat from my forehead with the back of my hand.

"*Grrrr!*" he said.

"What??" I said. "Back to the Nether?"

Cree shook his head, and spoke more insistently. "*Grrrr!*" he repeated.

"You know, one of these days, I'll have to learn that language you *mobs* speak in. But *yeah* ... that's right!" I said, remembering. "We still have that glowstone! We need to do *something* with it! It did cost us quite a bit of trouble!"

Before I went back into my house, the Nether portal in the middle of the square caught my eye. The shimmering field of purple energy moving and shifting inside of the obsidian gateway made the part of town I could see *through* it look warped and twisted...

The villagers were standing around it, looking at it, confused and a bit taken. One of them tried to touch it, but chickened out and returned his hand to his robes.

I smiled.

"I know, buddy," I said to him from afar. "I was like that too."

I was sure he didn't hear me. The weird drone of the portal was loud!

It still amazed me that everything had *really* happened!

It was like a dream!

I walked into my house and looked around at my neat, sorted little world.

Everything was different, yet the same. But I wasn't afraid anymore. Yeah, I was still a little nervous, but I wasn't *scared*, and that was an *awesome* feeling!

Cree walked in and nudged me out of my thoughts.

"Hey, buddy! We had a pretty great adventure together, huh?" I said to him, patting him where his shoulder would be.

"Grrrr! Rrrr!"

"Yeah, we were pretty brave, huh?" I said to him.

It was late in the afternoon.

We ate, and went back outside with the glowstone. I wanted to make something with the dust to *accent* my house...

After spending some time at my crafting table, I mounted my new glowstones on several tall pillars around the front of the house and in the yard.

When the sun finally set, the new lights were *beautiful!*

The growling of the mobs in the forest outside the village didn't scare me anymore, and I pulled up a chair to sit and admire my new lighting.

Cree sat with me on the front porch.

With my sword, armor, and Cree by my side, nothing could stop me...

Day 14

"Hey!" Alex said.

I startled, dropping the trowel I was using to plant some flowers.

"Whoa! Hey, yourself!" I said to her, picking up the tool and setting it up against the house.

"*Grrrr!*" Cree said to her.

"Hey, Cree!" she responded with a smile.

Alex walked up to me and dropped something at my feet.

It was big, with a weird shape, and made of leather...

What was it? I had never seen something like it before.

When Alex studied my confused face, she laughed and spoke up. "It's a saddle," she said. "You know ... for a *horse?*"

I nodded. I still didn't know what that meant for me.

"Okay," I said.

"We're going to a place that's a few days travel from here," she said to me, "to get some horses!"

Cree looked at me and cocked his head.

He was wondering what I would do.

Alex sighed. "Steve, would you like to go?" she asked.

After pausing to think, and looking at Cree, I smiled.

"Yes," I said. "Yes, I would!"

Alex beamed and nodded. "Fantastic! Can't wait!"

Cree purred and *grrrr-ed*.

Everything had changed so much for me since I let this friendly creeper into my life.

Now, I wasn't scared of everything anymore, I had friends, and I wouldn't change it for the world!

"When do we leave?" I asked.

Want More Steve and Cree?

1. Please go to where you bought this book and *leave a review!* It just takes a minute and it really helps!

2. Join my free *Skeleton Steve Club* and get an email when the next book comes out!

3. Look for your name under my *"Amazing Readers List"* at the end of the book, where I list my *all-star reviewers*. Heck—maybe I'll even use your name in a story if you want me to! (*Let me know in the review!*)

About the Author - Skeleton Steve

I am *Skeleton Steve*, author of *epic* unofficial Minecraft books. *Thanks for reading this book!*

My stories aren't your typical Minecraft junkfood for the brain. I work hard to design great plots and complex characters to take you for a roller coaster ride in their shoes! Er ... claws. Monster feet, maybe?

All of my stories written by (just) me are designed for all ages—kind of like the Harry Potter series—and they're twisting journeys of epic adventure! For something more light-hearted, check out my "Fan Series" books, which are collaborations between myself and my fans.

Smart kids will love these books! Teenagers and nerdy grown-ups will have a great time relating with the characters and the stories, getting swept up in the struggles of, say, a novice Enderman ninja (Elias), or the young and naïve creeper king

(Cth'ka), and even a chicken who refuses to be a zombie knight's battle steed!

I've been *all over* the Minecraft world of Diamodia (and others). As an adventurer and a writer at heart, I *always* chronicle my journeys, and I ask all of the friends I meet along the way to do the same.

Make sure to keep up with my books whenever I publish something new! If you want to know when new books come out, sign up for my mailing list and the *Skeleton Steve Club*. **It's free!**

Here's my website:

www.SkeletonSteve.com

You can also 'like' me on **Facebook**: Facebook.com/SkeletonSteveMinecraft

And 'follow' me on **Twitter**: Twitter.com/SkeletonSteveCo

And watch me on **Youtube**: (Check my website.)

"Subscribe" to my Mailing List and Get Free Updates!

I *love* bringing my Minecraft stories to readers like you, and I hope to one day put out over 100 stories! If you have a cool idea for a Minecraft story, please send me an email at *Steve@SkeletonSteve.com*, and I might make your idea into a real book. I promise I'll write back. :)

Other Books by Skeleton Steve

The "Noob Mob" Books

Books about individual mobs and their adventures becoming heroes of Diamodia.

Diary of a Creeper King
Book 1
Book 2
Book 3
Book 4

Skeleton Steve – The Noob Years
Season 1, Episode 1 – *FREE!!*
Season 1, Episode 2
Season 1, Episode 3
Season 1, Episode 4
Season 1, Episode 5
Season 1, Episode 6
Season 2, Episode 1
Season 2, Episode 2
Season 2, Episode 3
Season 2, Episode 4
Season 2, Episode 5
Season 2, Episode 6
Season 2, Episode 6
Season 3, Episode 1
Season 3, Episode 2
Season 3, Episode 3
Season 3, Episode 4
Season 3, Episode 5
Season 3, Episode 6

Diary of a Teenage Zombie Villager
Book 1 – *FREE!!*
Book 2
Book 3
Book 4

Diary of a Chicken Battle Steed
Book 1
Book 2
Book 3
Book 4

Diary of a Lone Wolf
Book 1
Book 2
Book 3
Book 4

Diary of an Enderman Ninja
Book 1 – *FREE!!*
Book 2
Book 3

Diary of a Separated Slime – Book 1

Diary of an Iron Golem Guardian – Book 1

The "Skull Kids" Books

A Continuing Diary about the Skull Kids, a group of world-hopping players

Diary of the Skull Kids
Book 1 – *FREE!!*
Book 2
Book 3

The "Fan Series" Books

Continuing Diary Series written by Skeleton Steve *and his fans!* Which one is your favorite?

Diary of Steve and the Wimpy Creeper
Book 1
Book 2
Book 3

Diary of Zombie Steve and Wimpy the Wolf
Book 1 *COMING SOON*

The "Tips and Tricks" Books

Handbooks for Serious Minecraft Players, revealing Secrets and Advice

Skeleton Steve's Secret Tricks and Tips

Skeleton Steve's Top 10 List of Rare Tips

Skeleton Steve's Guide to the
First 12 Things I Do in a New Game

Get these books as for FREE!

(Visit www.SkeletonSteve.com to *learn more*)

Series Collections and Box Sets

Bundles of Skeleton Steve books from the Minecraft Universe. Entire Series in ONE BOOK.

Great Values! Usually 3-4 Books (sometimes more) for almost the price of one!

Skeleton Steve – The Noob Years – Season 1
Skeleton Steve – The Noob Years – Season 2

Diary of a Creeper King – Box Set 1

Diary of a Lone Wolf – Box Set 1

Diary of an Enderman NINJA – Box Set 1

Diary of the Skull Kids – Box Set 1

Steve and the Wimpy Creeper – Box Set 1

Diary of a Teenage Zombie Villager – Box Set 1

Sample Pack Bundles

Bundles of Skeleton Steve books from multiple series! New to Skeleton Steve? Check this out!

Great Values! Usually 3-4 Books (sometimes more) for almost the price of one!

Skeleton Steve and the Noob Mobs Sampler Bundle
Book 1 Collection
Book 2 Collection
Book 3 Collection
Book 4 Collection

-

Check out the website
www.SkeletonSteve.com
for more!

Enjoy this Excerpt from...

"Diary of an **Enderman Ninja**" Book 1

About the book:

Love MINECRAFT? ****Over 16,000 words of kid-friendly fun!****

This high-quality fan fiction fantasy diary book is for **kids, teens, and nerdy grown-ups** who love to read *epic stories* about their favorite game!

Elias was a young Enderman. And he was a NINJA.

As an initiate of the Order of the Warping Fist, Elias is sent on a mission by his master to investigate the deaths of several Endermen at Nexus 426. Elias is excited to prove himself as a novice martial artist, but is a little nervous--he still hasn't figured out how to dodge arrows!

And now, when the young Enderman ninja discovers that the source of the problem is a trio of tough, experienced Minecraftian players, will he be in over his head? And what's this talk about a 'Skeleton King' and an army of undead?

Love Minecraft adventure??

Read on for an Excerpt for the book!

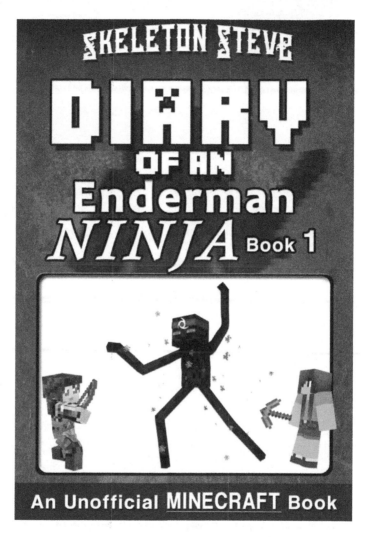

SKELETON STEVE

DIARY
OF AN
Endeman
NINJA Book 1

An Unofficial MINECRAFT Book

Day 1 - Overworld

When I teleported to the Overworld, I never thought that I would be starting a *diary*.

It is always interesting, the adventures that life puts in my path. So here I am, an Enderman, sitting on a rock and penning words into this empty book I found in a chest.

The day is clear today. Warm. Very pleasant.

It feels strange, trying to think of things to say with my fingers instead of with my mind, to use this archaic quill and ink to put words on paper.

The grass, and the leaves in the trees, are swaying and whispering in the wind, as I scratch these words onto paper in this leather-bound book resting on my lap.

Such is the way.

I am reminded frequently by the flow of the world around me to ignore my expectations, because once I expect something to go *one* way, the universe opens like a flower and teases me into another direction.

But I am ninja, so I flow like water.

Or, at least, I *try* to.

So I embrace this journal. This diary.

I will write of my adventures on my *Seed Stride*, and it will become part of my way. A painting of this path on my journey of life.

My name is Elias, and I am Ender.

I am also an initiate in the Order of the Warping Fist—a unique group of Endermen *ninja*. By now, I would have normally been granted the title of 'lower ninja', but the end of my initiate training was interrupted by the Seed Stride.

It occurs to me that writing this diary gives life to my story, and my story may travel on away from me once it has life. One day, my story and I may go separate ways—my body and my words separate, but together.

So I must explain.

The 'Seed Stride' is a rite of passage for young Endermen. Just before we reach adulthood and become full members of the Ender race, we are compelled to go on a Seed Stride. This is the first of many Seed Strides I will take over the course of my life, to help contribute to the well-being and expansion of my people.

We Ender, as a race, rely on the Pearls, our *Chi*, to produce more Ender, and to attune ourselves to the rhythm of the universe. Our Chi is also the source of our power to teleport, to warp between worlds, and also enhances our ability to communicate by the voice of the mind.

Such things we Ender take for granted. But it is possible that *you*, whoever picks up this book, as my story decides to *travel* later, may not understand the simple concepts that I've known since my birth.

So, now that you understand, *know* that my first Seed Stride was the reason my initiate ninja training was interrupted before completion.

Mature Endermen all understand, either through training or experience, how to dodge arrows and other missile weapons through the

242

awareness they achieve by being in tune with their *Chi* and the world around them.

I'm still working on it.

When it was time to begin my Seed Stride, I was a little concerned that I hadn't yet mastered the Chi dodge, but as a ninja, I am comfortable enough in my combat ability to make up for my lack of skill in Chi.

Once my Seed Stride is complete, I will return to my master to complete my training. Then, I will increase in rank to lower ninja and start participating in real missions.

I understand that I am supposed to control my emotions. But the idea of finally being a real ninja and going on missions for the Order excites me! I'm sure that such excitement clouds my mind with impatience...

But I've got that impatience under control—really, I do!

So, I mentioned that the Ender people rely on the pearls. The pearls are the source of our enhanced power; the technology of our race.

I received my Ender pearl when I was very small. After going through the trials like all Ender younglings, I was chosen for the order. Some Endermen are more naturally in tune with their Chi than others. My connection and potential showed that I would be one of the few chosen to protect and further the race.

And now, I was almost fully-grown.

Though I recognize the value of humility, I was confident in my strengths.

I'm strong. And fast. And my martial arts skill is among the highest in my class.

I was sure that my connection with my Chi would catch up.

But I was out of time.

The time of my Seed Stride had come, so my training was paused, and now I am sitting on a rock in the sun, being one with the wind and the grass, and writing in this book...

Earlier today, I found a jungle.

The tall, green trees and lush ground was a most interesting biome! There were pools of water here and there, and I realized that a place so green had to experience frequent rain.

Warping through the environment, searching for pearl seeds in the dirt under thick vegetation, I knew that I needed to stay sharp—I wouldn't want to get caught in the rain!

But it didn't rain.

And I found *four* pearl seeds in dirt blocks during the time I traveled and warped through the interesting and lush environment. Trying to sense the Ender energy within, I picked up and discarded block after block of dirt until I could feel the pull of the Chi inside.

Whenever I found a dirt block containing a pearl seed, I opened my dimensional pocket, and stored the block with the other seed blocks for my return home.

The dirt blocks I collected would stay inside the dimensional pocket until I returned to the End at the completion of my Seed Stride.

There was no requirement or limit on the amount of blocks an Enderman was expected to collect on a Seed Stride. Finding the pearl seeds for our people was something engrained in us from an early age—something we were expected to do as a service to our race.

I figured that I would know when I had collected enough seeds. My heart was open, and I would listen to my instinct. Once I finished this Seed Stride, and was satisfied with my service to the Ender people, I would return to the End to plant my seeds and continue my ninja training.

Some Endermen collected more seeds than others. And some dedicated their *entire lives* to the Seed Stride, walking the Overworld forever in search of the dirt blocks that held the promise of a growing pearl.

I would work hard, and collect many seeds. My life as a member of the Order was sworn to a duty to the people, after all. But my real goals lay in the path to becoming a better ninja.

I loved being a ninja. And once I rose to the rank of a lower ninja, I would at least have the respect of my peers.

Yes, maybe I suffered from a *little* bit of pride. I was aware.

But I knew what I wanted.

I wanted to be the best.

The strongest and fastest ninja. I wanted to be a shadow. In time, I hoped that I could even become a master, and be able to channel my Chi into fireballs, and do all of the other cool ninja stuff that Master Ee-Char could do.

So far, I had twenty-seven seeds. Pausing to peer into my dimensional pocket, I counted them again. Twenty-seven blocks of dirt, all holding the promise of growing an Ender pearl to be joined with twenty-seven Ender younglings in the future.

Perhaps one of them would also become a ninja, like me.

When I was in the jungle, earlier today, I found an old structure. Old for *Minecraftians*, I guess.

The small building was made of chiseled stone blocks, now overrun with vines and green moss.

As I explored the inside of the old Minecraftian structure, I noted that it was some sort of *temple*. My ninja awareness easily detected a couple of rotting, crude traps, and I avoided the trip lines and pressure plates without effort.

Inside a wooden chest, among a bunch of Minecraftian junk and zombie meat, I found *this book*.

Out of curiosity, I experimented with the levers by the stairs, until I revealed a hidden room with another wooden chest. Just more junk. Pieces of metal and bones.

Those Minecraftians and their junk...

At least, I *figured* it was Minecraftian junk. I had never personally *met* one of the creatures before. From what I'd heard in my training and tales from other Endermen, the Minecraftians were small and weak, but were intelligent, and were able to transform the Overworld into tools, armor, and other technology that made them stronger.

The older Endermen told me stories about the famous *Steve*, as well as other Minecraftians that came and went frequently on the Overworld. We even saw a Minecraftian or two appear every once and a while on the dragon's island, stuck on our world because of dabbling with portal technology they didn't understand. I've never seen them myself, but I've heard about the incidents from Endermen who were there at the time.

Usually, the visiting Minecraftians had it out for the dragon.

It never lasted long.

Apparently, they were usually surprised when they appeared on the obsidian receiver, and realized that there was no way to get home! I've heard that when they inevitably decide to attack the dragon, the great, ancient beast just *plucks them up* and throws them out into the void.

Well, now I had a piece of their junk. This book was constructed from leather and paper, which was likely constructed from something else. This ink was created by Minecraftians as well—all components derived from plants, animals, and minerals of the Overworld, to be sure.

What a beautiful day!

This Overworld is very bright during the day—uncomfortably so. But it's very peaceful and lovely.

I think I'll meditate for a while and write more tomorrow...

Day 2 - Overworld

After meditating, filling my Chi, and exploring the Overworld during the night, I decided to stay out in the open again during the next day.

I ran into another couple of Endermen during the night, a time when exploring is a lot easier on our eyes. But now, during the day, now that the sunlight is flooding the world around me, I'm all alone again.

During my training, I was never told to only go out at night, but it seems to be an unspoken rule of my people on the Seed Stride here. And I can understand why. The sun was so bright and hot on my eyes! But I didn't care. Let the others go into hiding or warp back to the End during the day. I had *seeds* to collect and an infinite world to explore!

Today, I observed the animals and the Overworld's native mobs.

There were several different kinds of beasts that I found, as I teleported from valley to valley, hillside to hillside, as the sky lightened with the rising sun. White, clucking birds, fluffy sheep, spotted cows, pink pigs. I was able to understand them by using my Chi to perceive their thoughts, but their language was very basic and they mostly communicated with each other through grunts and noises.

"*What is your name?*" I asked a particular chicken with my *mind voice*.

"*I am a chicken*," it thought back. "Bawk!" it said aloud.

"What is your purpose?"

"I am eating."

The bird scratched at the ground with its goofy yellow feet, pulling plant seeds out of the tall grass.

As the morning went on, I noticed that some of the larger, more complicated creatures, the *mobs*, as I was taught they were called, *burst* into flames as the sun settled higher into the sky! Skeletons and zombies raced around, frantic and on fire, until they burned up and left behind nothing but piles of ash, bones, and charred meat.

What an interesting world.

As I teleported into the shadows of a tall, dark forest, I found a lone zombie hiding from the sun under a pine tree. He held a metal shovel in his hand—a Minecraftian tool.

"Excuse me," I said into his mind.

"Who…? Who's there?" the zombie asked in a dull, slow voice. The creature looked around with black eyes.

I stepped out from the shadows to where it couldn't help but notice me. It's not like I was *trying* to hide before—I don't know how it didn't see me.

The zombie's face stretched in surprise. "Oh!" it cried. "You surprised me! So sneaky!" It settled down, paused, and stood vacant for a moment before speaking again. "What you want?"

"I was wondering … why does the sun sets zombies on fire?" I said into its mind.

The zombie was shocked. "The sun sets zombies on *fire?!*" It was suddenly very aware of the sunlight just outside of the shadow of the tree, and the poor undead creature clutched at the pine's trunk to keep away from the light.

"*Elias,*" I suddenly heard in my mind. The voice of another Enderman. "*Behind you.*"

Turning, I saw, across a sunny valley, was an area of deep shadow under a cliff—probably a cave. Another Enderman stood inside. From here, I could see his eyes glowing purple in the dark, and I could barely make out the white symbol of the *Order of the Warping Fist* on his black headband.

Another ninja.

I left the zombie, teleporting across the valley to stand before the other Enderman.

"*What is it, sir?*" I asked. It was Erion, a lower ninja from the rank just above me. He had finished his initial training, and would now be expected to perform minor missions while still taking training from his master. His headband was black instead of blue (like mine), but still bore the white symbol of a novice.

Soon I would have a black headband like his.

"Elias, you have been summoned by Master Ee'char. He has ordered that you return to the Temple immediately."

"But … my Seed Stride…?"

"Master Ee'char is aware that you are on Seed Stride. He has sent me to find you and ask you to return to him, still." Erion broke eye contact for a moment, and glared around at the sunny valley. *"What are you doing exploring during the day?"*

"Thank you, Erion. I'll return directly," I said into his mind.

The other Enderman ninja nodded, then disappeared with a *zip* and a brief shower of tiny, purple motes of light.

I turned, and noticed that the zombie I was talking to was gone. In front of the tree, outside of the shadow and in the sunlight, was a pile of charred meat ... and a shovel.

Huh.

What a strange world.

Teleporting around on a single world was easy. It was a lot like making a long jump—didn't require much energy, much of my *Chi*. I could overdo it, of course. If I warped around too much in too short a period of time, I would ... get tired, in a way. If my energy became too low, I would have to wait, or meditate for a while, until I had enough Chi to teleport again.

While exploring during my Seed Stride, the more I practiced harnessing my Chi for warping, the more I could do it without resting. I suppose there would come a time when teleporting on one world like I did here—hill to hill, place to place—would become as easy as blinking my eyes. In time.

But not yet. I still had to try. Still had to focus. And I could still get tired.

Teleporting was easier today than it was yesterday, though. With practice, I'd be able to warp more without resting and recharging my Chi—I was sure of it!

Jumping to another world was a different matter, however.

Going back and forth between the Overworld and the End was difficult, and required me to focus and have very strong Chi. The act needed *all* of my energy. And I'd probably need to recharge quite a bit before I could do it again.

So I sat on the cool stone in the shadow of the cave mouth, my legs crossed, my hands open and resting on my knees, receptive to the Overworld's Ender energy.

I meditated for a while, and let my thoughts dissipate. Focused only on my breathing, I willed my body to be a *receiver* for the energy of the world—the combined energy of all of the pearl seeds hidden in the blocks around me ... the energy of the world's core. It all funneled into me, moving up my arms, my legs, spiraling to my center ... to my *Chi*.

My Ender pearl was warm inside of me.

And I warped home.

CURRENTLY FREE!!

Enjoy this Excerpt from...

"Diary of a **Creeper King**" Book 1

About the book:

Ever heard of the **Creeper King**, mighty Cth'ka?

Read the adventure diary of a young creeper who was looking for a way to protect himself without *blowing up*!

When Cth'ka the Creeper and Skeleton Steve leave the forest to ask the local witch for help, they are soon on a long and dangerous journey to find a **secret artifact** that will allow Cth'ka the power to move blocks *with his mind*! But will the difficulty of traveling across the Minecraft world, a village under attack, hiding from a fully-armored killer hero, and finding the way to a hidden stronghold be too much for a creeper and his skeleton companion to handle?

Love Minecraft adventure??

Read on for an Excerpt for the book!

Day 1

Let's see ... is this '*Night* 1' or '*Day* 1'? I figure I'll write these entries in terms of *days*, since I never sleep. I will try to ignore the fact that, since I don't have hands that I can write with, I'm sitting under a tree right now *dictating*, saying my story out loud, to my good friend, Skeleton Steve.

He says that I should just tell the story like I'm writing it. I'll give this a try.

My name is Cth'ka. I'm a creeper. I don't know if that's the *real* name of my race, but that's what everyone calls us, so it works.

Other creepers would probably say that I'm a weird guy. An oddball.

But other creepers don't say much.

That's what's different about me. I don't know very much about where we came from. Heck, I don't even remember much about a year or so ago.

How did I get here? As far as I know, I've always lived in this forest. Skeleton Steve calls it "Darkwood Forest". He says that there are hundreds—*thousands* of other forests, so he likes to give names to places.

I do love this place.

The hills rise and fall, and the trees are thick, tall, and dark. *Dark oak*, Steve says. It's a very large forest too. I've never felt much of an urge to leave.

On one side of the forest, where the hills slope down, there's a thick jungle where the trees are different. On another side, the hills rise higher and higher until the trees stop, and snowy peaks reach into the sky.

I never go there, to the cold mountains. Hardly ever, really. I prefer to be in warmer places.

The jungle is nice and warm, but it's also full of water and rivers, and I don't care for water—not at all.

On the other sides of Darkwood forest, the hills continue for quite a ways with tall, dark oak trees, until they wind down into some grassy plains full of flowers and horses.

I love this forest, but I'm getting side-tracked.

Creepers are very solitary. I've seen many creatures in this world, living in and passing through my forest. Some creatures have moms and dads. Most of them are babies and then grow up.

The zombies and skeletons don't. I don't know where *they* come from. Where Skeleton Steve came from. I think he was something else before he became who he is today.

I don't know much about my past. Or where my race came from.

I don't remember having a mom or dad. And I don't remember being smaller, or growing up in any way. I hope to find out about these things in time.

Creepers don't exactly have a library of their race's past. There's nothing to study. Nothing we can learn from our elders. I can't even tell the difference between a young creeper and an old creeper! I assume that I'm young, but maybe we just don't have very good memories. Who knows?

And the creepers I see while I walk around my forest don't have much to say either.

Earlier today, I was in my favorite part of Darkwood. My *clearing*. Near the very middle of this forest is a large clearing, a place where the trees break, and a wide valley of grass stretches out a long way. Red and yellow flowers pepper the open expanse. I love to go there during the day and watch the flowers sway in the breeze, feel the sun on my skin, and watch the clouds roll by.

At the time, Skeleton Steve was back in the forest. He doesn't sleep either, but he can't explore with me during the day. If Skeleton Steve steps into the sunlight ... *foom*! He'd catch on fire. I've only seen it happen once before—he's pretty careful. But I guess that's just part of being undead.

So Skeleton Steve was back in the thickest part of the forest, waiting out the day in the shadow of a large dark oak tree, and I was watching another creeper walk across the clearing.

Whenever I see another creeper, I always try to make conversation, to learn about them. It's always my hope to learn more about my people, and to make friends who are like me.

"Hi there," I said.

The other creeper noticed me, said nothing, then turned to continue moving away. I followed.

"My name is Cth'ka. What's yoursss?"

The other creeper stopped, and turned to face me. "What you wantsss?"

"I don't sssee othersss like me very often. Where did you come from? Where are you going?"

"What doesss it matter to you?" he said in a gravelly voice. He turned, and continued walking through the valley.

"I jussst want to be friendsss," I said to his back. "Pleassse tell me about yourssself!"

I stopped.

The other creeper kept moving, without speaking again, and I stood in the sun and watched until he disappeared into the shadows of the dark oak trees.

Later that day, when the sun went down, I walked back to where I knew Skeleton Steve was waiting for me. In the shadows of the darkening forest, I could see the glowing red dots of his eyes, hovering in the middle of his empty black eye sockets, watching me approach.

"Why do you always try to talk to the other creepers?" Skeleton Steve asked after I told him about my day. "They always act the same way."

We were walking along a ridge, watching the moon rise into the sky. Skeleton Steve's face was silver in the fading light. I could see in the darkness just fine, but when the light faded away, the colors of the world disappeared too. I did love the daylight, when everything was bold and colorful. It was too bad that Skeleton Steve always had to hide in the dark.

"I've got to try," I said. "There have to be more creepersss out there like me. I want to know more about why we're here. How we creepersss *get* here."

"So many creepers are just ... grumpy, it seems," Skeleton Steve said.

We walked in silence for a while.

"I wonder if we're ssstuck like thisss, or if there will ever be sssomeone to bring usss together. If there are other creepersss, sssmart like me, I'm sure we can do *great* thingsss."

"Why are you so interested in other creepers?" Skeleton Steve said.

"I think ... it would be a good thing for usss to come together," I said. I wasn't quite sure what I was getting at, but I knew that I wanted creepers, as a *people*, to find strength together somehow. To have a real race, a real history. Something unique that we could pass down to whatever it meant to be the next generation. I didn't even know if creepers had children, or how more creepers came to be. "We could maybe be—I don't know—a *real race*. Develop oursssselvesss instead of jussst being like animalsss wandering around all alone."

"You mean like creeper cities? A creeper nation?" Skeleton Steve said, smirking.

"I don't know," I said. "I jussst feel like, we could be … more."

Day 2

I stayed with Skeleton Steve in the dark during the day. We were close to the jungle, and I thought it might be fun to walk along the border when the sun went down. We might even see some areas of the jungle that were dry enough to let us walk down into it for a while without having to cross any *water*.

It would be nice to feel the warmth of the tropical forest. I hadn't visited the jungle in a long time.

Another creeper passed by, and I was at least able to get his name. Car'nuk. But we didn't talk about much else. I tried to find out how old Car'nuk was, and where he lived, but, like all of the others, he scowled at me, and went on his way.

It was a little sad, how difficult it was to communicate with my people. It's like we creepers were designed to never have anything to do with each other. And that was a pity. Creepers are natural-born explorers. We walk, all day and all night, and I'm sure there would be *plenty* to talk about if the others like me weren't so grumpy about having conversations.

When the sun went down, Skeleton Steve and I walked to the next ridge over, where we could look down into the jungle. Even in the fading light, I was surprised at how *green* the area was.

Some of the trees were squat and so thick that it made it hard to see the ground beneath them, and they were covered with vines that descended like green, ropy sheets from the treetops. Other trees were massive and tall, popping out of the canopy with large clumps of leaves extending in multiple directions.

I bet it rained a lot here.

It was hard to see through the trees, but I could see water here and there, down below. There must be rivers and pools *all over*.

I could never live in the jungle. I don't like the water. Never have. I've always had a hard time with the idea of floating in the water, even though I've seen other creepers swim before—I don't know how to ssswim, and didn't know if I'd ever be able to figure it out.

With my little legs, the idea of not being able to keep my head out of water, the idea of sssplashing and ssstruggling to get back to sssolid ground …. my lungsss filling up with water …. Ssssssssss … ssssssssssplashing, sssssssstruggling …

No thanksss. Just the *thought* of being stuck in water gets me all … excited. I've always thought it would be better to avoid water altogether.

As Skeleton Steve and I walked along the ridge, we looked out over the expanse of trees into the dense jungle below. The ridge descended gently into an area of jungle that wasn't as thick.

I hesitated.

"It's okay," Skeleton Steve said. "I don't see anything bad in there. It's just *part* jungle. Do you want to see what it looks like inside?"

I walked with him down into the tree-line. Darkwood Forest was behind us now, just on the other side of the ridge. There were no rivers or pools in the immediate area. No water.

We stood, peering into the depths of the jungle, and I was thinking about heading back to the forest when I saw movement! Green.

Another *creeper*!

I saw the distinct shape, its head turn, a face like mine looking back at us from the darkness for just a moment before it turned again.

"Hey!" I shouted. "Hello there!"

The creeper stood still, then turned to look at us again.

"Let'sss go in!" I said.

Skeleton Steve shrugged, and followed me deeper into the jungle.

We approached the creeper, and I called out to him again from a distance. "Hi there, fellow creeper! I'm Cth'ka! Do you live here in the jungle?"

As we continued making our way to my new friend through the heavy underbrush, I saw the creeper suddenly snap his attention to one side, then stagger back a few steps. I could hear him *hiss*, unsure at first, then again—intensely! The creeper fell back again, and I saw something on its chest—a *blur* of a creature, dim without color, but ... *spots*?

The creeper was under attack?!

I was suddenly afraid, and faintly heard Skeleton Steve, at my side, pull out his bow and nock an arrow. The creeper hissed again, a continual, rising, sputtering sound! It was definitely an animal of some kind, a spotted creature, small, clawing and biting at my intended friend.

"Ocelot!" Skeleton Steve said.

Expanding and shaking, hissing even louder, the creeper suddenly *exploded* with a thunderous *boom!*

What?! *How*?

How did that ...?

Shocked, I stood, staring at the spot where the creeper and the ocelot were fighting, now a crater of raw dirt and shredded plants, and I felt fear wash over me again when I saw two white and yellow forms darting through the bushes ... straight at *me*.

Two more ocelots! Little greens eyes, focused on me.

"Run!" Skeleton Steve yelled, and I stumbled backwards as an arrow suddenly struck one of the cats. It turned and sprinted off to Steve.

As I focused on the ocelot about to attack me, trying to force my body turn and run away back up the hill, my *hearing* seemed to tighten around my heartbeat, my vision darkened around the edges, and Skeleton Steve's shouted warnings suddenly seemed very far away...

The ocelot leapt through the air at me, and I felt its claws and teeth sink into my body. I tried to turn and run, but it was hanging onto me. My hearing, now weird and hollow like I was in a deep cave, was focusing more and more on a ... hissing sound ... I ssscrambled, tried to essscape, tried to call for Ssskeleton Sssteve ... Ssssssssss ...

"Sssteve!   Sssssssssssssssssssssssssssssave
me!"

An arrow appeared out of nowhere sssticking out of the ocelot'sss ssside, and the cat fell. I turned and sssaw Ssskeleton Sssteve nocking another arrow, aiming past me.

I ran up the hill. Turned. Sssaw Ssskeleton Sssteve kill the ocelot. He ran to catch up to me, his bonesss rattling.

We ran back up the hill out of the jungle together, back up to the ridge.

"Are you okay?" Skeleton Steve said.

I could suddenly hear again, see again, like normal!

"Yesss," I said. "What … ssssssssss …. What happened?"

Skeleton Steve sat on the ridge, looking out over the jungle, his bow still in his hand.

"Those were ocelots," he said. "Mostly harmless animals. Strange that they attacked. Usually they mind their own business. I know they don't like creepers, but I've never seen them *attack* one before."

"What happened to the creeper?" I asked. "It *blew up!*"

Skeleton Steve looked at me. "You don't know?" he asked.

I shook my head.

Skeleton Steve's glowing red dots of eyes looked me over. "That—blowing up—that's what creepers *do*. They explode. In self-defense, and also when they're attacking a *Steve*."

"When they're attacking *you?*"

"No," Skeleton Steve said. "A *Steve*." He looked off at the moon. "My name is Steve, yes, but there is another creature on this world named 'Steve' as well. He's different than us."

"But why *explode?*" I said.

"That's all that the creeper *could* do," Skeleton Steve said. "When the ocelot attacked him, he exploded in self-defense, and killed it."

I was so confused. Why would he defend himself … by killing himself?

"It doesn't make sssenssse," I said.

Skeleton Steve looked at me. "No one knows why creepers explode, Cth'ka. There's no other way for them to defend themselves, really. And I've never seen a creeper really *care*. I've seen creepers launch themselves at Steve and happily blow up in his face!" He regarded me for a moment. "*You* were about to explode too, you know. When that ocelot attacked you? I'm surprised you didn't, actually."

I looked down at my body, at the wounds where the cat had ripped at me.

So *that's* what that was—when I was losing concentration, when my vision and my hearing changed. Was I preparing to blow myself up?

"Why didn't I explode?" I asked.

"I don't know," Skeleton Steve said. "Maybe you're a little different? Maybe with how *smart* you are, compared to other creepers I've seen, you're able to control yourself better? We'll have to look into that some more—so you can survive longer. I'd hate to lose you as my friend, if you ever get attacked again and blow up, or if we run into the *Steve*."

What a twist to my pleasant little life, roaming around in my forest! I had never seen a creeper explode before. I didn't even know it was possible. And now, there was a way that, if I was freaked out enough, I could lose control of my mind and blow myself up, too?

No way! That's crazy. I had a life to live. I wanted to bring 'creeperkind' together and learn more about our race. To learn more about our past and our culture … if there was one. Surely there was more to the creeper race than random solitary creatures that avoid having friends and then eventually blow themselves up?

What could I do?

I was defenseless. If Skeleton Steve wasn't with me, I would have been helpless, and killed by those ocelots. Or turned myself into a living bomb and ended up *dead* just the same.

"How can I defend myssself?" I muttered.

We sat quietly for a few moments. The tall grass swayed in the night breeze.

"I have an idea," Skeleton Steve said. He was watching me as I sat, thinking. "*You* are special, Cth'ka. I'd like to see you learn to control your 'defense mechanism' and be able to defend yourself properly, but you can't use weapons like me, and you can't run very fast. We should go and talk to the witch! Maybe she'll have an idea."

"Witch?" I asked.

"Yes," Steve said. "There's a witch not too far from here, named Worla. I've dealt with her in the past, and she's very clever. She might be able to figure out why you're different. Maybe she'll have an idea about how to make it *easier* for you to survive without blowing yourself up one day."

For the rest of the night, Skeleton Steve and I traveled to the edge of the forest that was closest to the swamp. Before the sun came up, we found a small cave, and decided to wait out the day in there.

Day 3

When the sun went down, and undead could walk around outside safely again, we departed for the witch.

Standing at the edge of the forest, I could feel Darkwood behind me like a warm, safe hug, and the plains stretching out ahead of us, the empty rolling hills in the distance were ... unknown.

We struck out, down from the shadows of the dark oak trees, into green and yellow fields. A group of horses of different colors stood quietly in the grass far off to the left, staying still in the night. A couple of zombies roamed aimlessly in the valley nearby.

"So, over those hills ahead," Skeleton Steve said, "is a swamp where Worla lives."

"A ssswamp?" I said. "Like, full of ... water?"

Skeleton Steve laughed.

"Yes," he said. "Swamps are full of water. But that's where *witches* live."

"Can't we just have her come to usss?"

Skeleton Steve looked back at me while we walked. "Cth'ka, sometimes, to get good things, you have to take *risks*."

We walked across the great, open valley, then up into some sparse hills, as the wind whistled across the plain and the moon slowly moved across the sky. The hills were mostly devoid of trees at first, then started sprouting white trees here and there. Skeleton Steve called them 'Birch' trees. The hills rolled on, with more and more trees, until we seemed to be heading downhill all the time, and the trees turned darker.

Eventually, vines started growing from the trees, then further on, thick *sheets* of vines cascaded down their sides, a lot like the trees we saw in the jungle. The ground flattened out, and we were suddenly standing at the edge of a huge swamp, with random dirt and mud and water alternating as far as I could see, full of weeping trees. The air was hot and wet, and large lily pads spotted the surface of the water.

"That'sss a *lot* of water," I said.

"It's okay," Skeleton Steve said. "We'll stay on land where we can, and you can use the lily pads when you need to."

Lily pads? A sssaucer of *plant stuff* being the only thing keeping me from drowning in the murky water of this dreadful place?

"Where'sss the witch?" I said.

"Worla's hut is a little ways past that outcropping of rock over there," Skeleton Steve said, pointing to a spire of rock sticking out of a small hill, deep in the swamp.

Over the next few hours, we traveled across the bog. There was a *lot* of water, but Skeleton Steve was right! He was careful in planning where to walk, and planning ahead, and we stayed on dry ground most of the time. There were a few places where I had to cross water, but we were able to avoid swimming by finding areas where the land was close together, and joined with lily pads.

Once we reached the spire landmark, Skeleton Steve pointed deeper into the swamp, and I saw, in the fog, a small, dark dwelling standing on wooden stilts. The light of a fire inside made the hut stand out in the darkness.

"I've never ssseen a witch before," I said.

"Just be respectful, and certainly stay calm!" Skeleton Steve said with a smile.

When we approached the little building, I was relieved to see that it was mostly on land. I was afraid that I would have to cross more lily pads or even try to cross open water to get there. A rickety wooden ladder was lashed to one of the stilts, and it led to the deck on the front of the little house, and standing on the deck...

"Who goes there?" a woman's twisted and sharp-edged voice rang out in the quiet, dark night.

I saw a strange creature standing on the deck, just outside the doorway, her body wrapped in a dark purple robe, her hands hidden inside, and a black cowl hid most of her face. Her features were angry, and a hook-like nose curled down in front of a scowling mouth.

"Reveal your intentions," she said, "or I'll set you on *fire*!"

"Worla!" my bony friend said, "It is I, Skeleton Steve, and my companion, Cth'ka, come to consult your wisdom!"

She seemed to think for a moment.

"Skeleton Steve," she said, her voice suddenly much more friendly. "*You* are welcome, but I cannot risk your creeper companion destroying my home! I'll be down directly. Have a seat." She disappeared back into her doorway.

Skeleton Steve smirked at me. He looked around the clearing where we stood, and walked over to a circle of fallen logs. He sat on a log.

I followed.

A few minutes later, the witch descended her ladder with ease, and approached us. She sat on a log opposite Skeleton Steve so that we could all speak. A torch stuck out of the ground in the middle of our circle, which I didn't notice before, and it *flared* to life, casting fiery reflections and dancing shadows all around us.

"I am Worla," she said to me, "the witch of Lurkmire Swamp."

"I am Cth'ka," I said, "creeper ... of Darkwood Foressst?"

Skeleton Steve laughed. Worla laughed. I relaxed.

"What can *my wisdom* do for you tonight, Skeleton Steve?" she said.

"We've come because of my creeper friend here, Cth'ka," he said. "He is on a quest to learn more about his race, and to bring his people together, but is in need of a way to *defend* himself without blowing himself up."

Worla cackled. "A creeper trying to *avoid* blowing himself up?"

"Why isss that ssso funny?" I asked, my tone a little harsher than I intended. Skeleton Steve flinched a little.

"Because," the witch said, "creepers are quite *happy* to blow themselves up. It's their *destiny*. It's how they make *more* creepers."

What?

"Sssssss ... *More* creepersss?" I said. That was absurd!

"Look into my eyes, young creeper. Let me look into your *destiny*." She leaned forward toward me.

I looked at Skeleton Steve. He shrugged. Looking back at Worla the witch, I took a deep breath, steadied my fear, and held still, looking right into her beady, black eyes. In the flickering flames of the torchlight, I saw my frowning, green face reflected back at me in her eyes. Worla's face was still and passive, then it transformed in surprise!

"Oh my," she said, her black eyes unmoving but her face animating around them. "My, my. What an *interesting* path you have, mighty Cth'ka..."

Mighty?

She continued. "I can see what lies ahead for you, most interesting creeper. Interesting, indeed!"

"What isss?" I asked.

"Yeah," Skeleton Steve said. "What's so interesting?"

Worla laughed, breaking her eyes out of the dark and stony stare that held my own eyes in a tight grip. My attention to the swamp around me suddenly snapped back into focus.

"Cth'ka the creeper," she said. "I *will* help you, yes. I will tell you the location of an ... *artifact* of sorts, something that will allow you the ability to act with *hands unseen*, strong hands that will let you *smash* your enemies and defend yourself without using your ... last resort. Is this idea to your liking?"

I had no idea what she meant by all of that. Hands unseen? Some kind of weird magic?

"What do you mean?" I said. "Handsss unssseen?"

"Yes," she replied. "A magical item that will let you manipulate the world around you with your *mind*. The only possible defense for someone of your kind, assuming you don't want to destroy yourself."

She waved her hand, and the torch snuffed out like magic. A snap of her long, spindly fingers, and it flared to life again.

"I will give you items to assist in your journey as well. I only ask a small price in return..."

"What price?" I said.

"I am ... building my interest here in Lurkmire still, and will require your assistance in the future. I ask for three favors upon your return with the artifact, and in exchange, I will give you the knowledge and ability to attain the power to fulfill your destiny and *lead your people*."

Everything I wanted.

But at what price?

What could the witch possible ask of me that I wouldn't be able to give her, especially once I had the power to manipulate the world with my mind and bring my people together in a nation of creeperkind?

I looked to Skeleton Steve. He returned my gaze without emotion.

He wasn't going to help me with *this* decision.

Wasn't this kind of idea what we traveled here for in the first place? Could I trust Worla the witch? If I asked Steve for his opinion, I would basically be asking him whether or not he thought I could trust the witch. I might offend her, and she might change her mind about the whole thing!

306

"Okay, I'll do it!" I said. "I'll get the artifact, then help you with your three favors."

She instantly pulled her hands out of her robe, her fingers like white spider legs in the darkness, tipped with thin claws. "Say it again," she commanded. "Repeat—I, Cth'ka the creeper, in exchange for assistance in finding the *Crown of Ender*, will perform three favors for Worla the Witch when she requires in the future."

I repeated her words, and she traced patterns in the darkness with her fingertips as I did. When I completed the sentence, she lashed out with her index finger, and touched my forehead. I flinched in surprise, caught control of my hissssssss, and felt a warm sensation bloom between my eyes then disappear.

Some sort of magic?

"You are unique, creeper," she said. "You will learn to control your *last resort* with your willpower. I can sense that already you can calm yourself back down. In time, you will be able to fight your enemies while keeping your mind calm, and not have to worry about exploding at all!"

Her hands disappeared back into her robes, then she produced three greenish-blue and yellow spheres. When she held out her palm to show us, the three spheres floated above her hand, throwing off purple motes of light. In the center of each sphere was a black slit of a pupil. They were *eyes*. Weird, magical eyeballs.

"These are eyes of Ender." She looked to Skeleton Steve. "Use them wisely. They will show you the way to the underground stronghold where you will find the Crown of Ender. Use one at a time, and *only* when you need to find the way. They will burn out in time. Follow the eyes to the location of the stronghold."

"Thank you," he said. Skeleton Steve took the eyes and put them into his pack.

"Remember," she said. "Only use them when you need to. Don't squander them!" She stood, pulling her robes about her. "And take care crossing the desert, my skeleton friend!" Worla laughed, and pulled the black cowl over her face again. The torch went out. "Good luck, mighty Cth'ka. Return to me once you have obtained the *crown*." She looked at the sky. "The night will soon be over..."

With that, Worla turned, and moved back to her hut with a speed and dangerous grace that I wouldn't have imagined.

I looked at Skeleton Steve. "I guesss we're ssstaying out of Darkwood Foressst for a while?"

He nodded, and we traveled back the way we came, stopping to spend the day under a large tree at the edge of the swamp.

Diary of a Steve and the Wimpy Creeper
Full Trilogy

CHECK OUT
SKELETONSTEVE.COM
... to CONTINUE READING!

The Amazing Reader List

Thank you SO MUCH to these Readers and Reviewers! Your help in leaving reviews and spreading the word about my books is SO appreciated!

Awesome Reviewers:

MantisFang887 EpicDrago887

ScorpCraft SnailMMS WolfDFang

LegoWarrior70

Liam Burroughs

Ryan / Sean Gallagher

Habblie

Nirupam Bhagawati

Ethan MJC

Jacky6410 and Oscar

MasterMaker / Kale Aker

Cole

Kelly Nguyen

Ellesea & Ogmoe

K Mc / AlfieMcM

JenaLuv & Boogie

Han-Seon Choi

Danielle M

Oomab

So Cal Family

Daniel Geary Roberts

Jjtaup

Addidks / Creeperking987

D Guz / UltimateSword5

TJ

Diary of a Steve and the Wimpy Creeper
Full Trilogy

Xavier Edwards

DrTNT04

UltimateSword5

Mavslam

Ian / CKPA / BlazePlayz

Dana Hartley

Shaojing Li

Mitchell Adam Keith

Emmanuel Bellon

Melissa and Jacob Cross

Wyatt D and daughter

Jung Joo Lee

Dwduck and daughter

Yonael Yonas, the Creeper Tamer (Jesse)

Sarah Levy / shadowslayer1818

Pan

Phillip Wang / Jonathan55123

Ddudeboss

Hartley

Mitchell Adam Keith

L Stoltzman and sons

D4imond minc4rt

Bookworm_29

Tracie / Johnathan

Jeremyee49

Endra07 / Samuel Clemens

And, of course ... Herobrine

(More are added all the time! Since this is a print version of this book, check the eBook version of the latest books—or the website—to see if your name is in there!)

Made in the USA
Las Vegas, NV
28 April 2022

48111128R00187